The Bird At The End Of Time

a novella

Scott Neil

Elvin Books

www.scottneilauthor.com

This edition has been published with US-English spelling.

A catalogue record of this book is available from the British Library.

The Bird At The End Of Time / Scott Neil -- 1st ed.

ISBN 978-1-7392428-1-7 (Hardback)

ISBN 978-1-7392428-0-0 (paperback)

ISBN 978-1-7392428-2-4 (ebook)

CHAPTER ONE

MANHATTAN

In space there is no sound. Now it was true on Earth.

That thought preyed on Commander Anna's mind as she watched a thin snake of sand whispering along the sidewalk, its fragile beauty disintegrating in the fading breeze. The sun's harsh brilliance bounced off the concrete; the heat oppressive in the still air. It was midday in Arizona. No dogs barked, no birds sang and not a single cicada chirped. Absolute silence was all in the deserted town.

'What have we done?' she asked. Her white flight suit clung tightly as she twisted to gaze up and down the desolate high street. In her mind she could still picture the bustling thoroughfare it had once been in her childhood vacations. She dragged a finger through dust and grains of sand coating a store window, and studied her ghostly reflection. The grime-covered glass dimmed the image of her uniform. On her left sleeve the space agency logo was unreadable, and below it an old flag of the United States of America still featured fifty stars, representing the states that had existed before the wars. Feeling light-headed she flinched and turned, briskly retracing her steps along the street towards the parking lot where she had landed her scramjet. She entered the one-person craft via a ramp and hatch door beneath the fuselage. The hatch clunked as it sealed itself behind her.

'Prepare for final circumnavigation. Set course. Best speed,' she instructed Sheean.

'Auto-control engaged,' responded the female voice of the artificial intelligence computer.

Anna tightened straps that buckled her to the pilot seat. The scramjet rose vertically, clearing the townhouse rooftops until the only thing outside the cockpit window was clear blue sky. Pitching gently and turning southeast it roared away, its supersonic combustion ramjet accelerating it to Mach 10. Clouds and the curved landscape blurred as the scramjet reached the stratosphere's edge at 7,000 miles per hour. Pressed hard against the headrest, Anna had counted the ten thudding shockwaves.

Her mission to oversee the final exodus shuttles departing Earth was almost complete. In daily reconnaissance sorties she'd searched for signs of life or rogue AI activity. Those flights, along with searches by ground-based autonomous drones, had turned up nothing. The world was smothered by toxins, radioactive storms and runaway climate change. Billions had perished. Life in the seas, on land and in the air had been wiped out. The exodus flights had removed what remained of the population, along with a pitiful smattering of flora and fauna.

Rogue AIs had done all they could to destroy what was left of the human race and prevent the exodus flights from departing. Mankind's response had been electromagnetic pulse blasts that destroyed the AIs, but also decimated most of the remaining electronic-reliant infrastructure. The Earth was now a poisoned wasteland and soon to be put under total planetary quarantine - lifeless, out of bounds and unlikely to recover for centuries, perhaps millennia.

An alarm beeped twice.

'What is it, Sheean?' Anna asked.

'A weak life signal,' replied the AI.

'Show location.'

A digital map on the dashboard screen zoned in on a flashing red icon, pinpointing the signal.

'Manhattan. Are you sure?' Anna asked.

Sheean confirmed, and said the signal was undefined and barely registered on the sensors.

'Okay. Let's take a look,' said Anna.

The scramjet rocked gently as its speed and altitude rapidly fell. The world outside became clearer, the curvature of the Earth swiftly flattened.

A voice broke in on the com-link. 'This is Exodus Shuttle 45. Preparing for departure.'

On the flight console screen Anna saw the captain of the shuttle staring back. 'Are you the last?' she asked.

The captain nodded.

'Then depart when ready. I'm taking a final sweep of Manhattan.'

'Manhattan.' The captain shook his head. 'That zone's been off limits for years. Do you have authorization?'

'I am the authority down here,' Anna smiled. 'I'll see you at Alpha rendezvous. Safe flight.'

The captain returned a half-smile. 'It's a certified dead zone. They're not going to like you doing that.'

'They don't have to. As for it being a dead zone, I've picked up a faint life single from a ground drone.'

The captain's image flickered. 'Drones fizzle in dead zones. It's probably a malfunction. I'm surprised it was there,' he said. 'You haven't got long, commander. Global quarantine is almost complete. After that, zap; nothing gets in or out.'

Anna reached forward, ready to disengage the call. 'I'm well aware, captain. Tell Artemis Control I'll be departing before ....' Her voice trailed off. The screen went blank.

The scramjet had entered a semi-permanent, wildly gyrating weather system of toxic gas and embedded, minuscule metallic shards that hung over the dead zone. Warning lights tangoed across the flight panel as Anna gripped the central lever, steering the craft through a murky soup of lethal gases. It was one of hundreds of poisoned weather systems swirling deadly cocktails across the world. As the compact craft plunged through the darkness, she fixed her attention on a monitor that showed an electronic representation of the jagged, hidden city below. Dropping from the underbelly of the clouds, the scramjet glided into a dim, deserted metropolis, where skyscrapers formed urban trenches stretching for miles along abandoned lifeless streets.

Anna piloted to the middle of Eighth Avenue, landing at the exact coordinates from where the faint life signal had been identified.

She disembarked. Her face was almost obscured in the tinted visor helmet of a bulky exoskeleton suit. Her small body was enhanced by its frame, which added two feet to her height and almost the same to her girth. Its hydraulics and active mechanics provided leverage power ten times greater than her body alone. Even so, a feeling of vulnerability chilled her. She gripped a flare pistol - her makeshift firearm. Beyond those now boarding the final exodus shuttle she was, as far as she knew, the last uncontaminated human on Earth, alone in a decayed city and searching for something alive.

To her left there was movement on the debris-strewn street. It was a shape that resembled an overgrown, waist-high beetle. She cautiously approached, then lowered her pistol.

'Ground droid. Looks about finished. Maybe that signal was a malfunction after-all.' She poked a gloved finger against the dust-covered robot. It emitted a mechanical hum as it strained to drag itself forward. As she watched, Anna felt a clatter against the top of her helmet. She instinctively tumbled onto her back, firing two rounds upwards. The flares rocketed away, exploding in red plumes. She scrambled back onto her feet. A small object darted across the sky towards a nearby building. She regained her breath and lifted her pistol.

'Sheean. What was it?' she asked, aware that images of the object, recorded by four cameras mounted on her suit, would have been monitored by the scramjet's AI.

'A bird,' came the reply.

Simultaneously, the word bird momentarily appeared as a digital projection on the inside of the helmet's visor. Anna lowered her pistol and strode towards the building where the bird had flown. The huge doors were locked. There was a gap in the wall, but it was too small to pass through wearing an exoskeleton suit.

'Sheean. Can I breathe the air?'

'Oxygen variable. Restrict exposure.'

The exoskeleton suit opened, the helmet lifted and Anna stepped out. She unhooked the pistol thigh holster from the suit and strapped it to the leg of her body-hugging flight fatigues, then squeezed her lithe figure through the gap in the wall. It led into a cavernous lobby. A tiny sparrow nearby vibrated its wings and chirped, then flew away. Anna followed it and discovered a long flight of stairs descending into darkness. Pulling a small torch from a side pocket, she used its narrow beam to guide her down the stairs. Another three flights followed, until she found herself standing on the dimly lit platform of a New York metro station. Ceiling-mounted emergency strip lights provided subdued illumination. The sparrow perched on a row of plastic seats set flush against a wall. Anna switched off the torch and held out her right hand, hoping the curious bird would land on her outstretched fingers. It flew away, spooked by a movement in the shadows. Anna spun around to face a dark, humanoid figure.

'Who are you?' she asked, sliding the pistol from its holster and pointing it at the figure walking towards her. 'Are you an AI?'

'Yes,' the robot replied. 'But I'm not one of … *them*.'

It was now ten feet away, its features clearer. It was a Sym-54 droid, one of the most widely used humanoid AIs. The rogue AIs that blitzed the surviving human population after the wars were all Sym-54s. Some of them were elaborate creations, almost indistinguishable from humans, while others, like this one, were basic metallic models.

Anna's nerves tingled. 'Stay where you are,' she ordered. 'The bird. How is it still alive?'

A reply came, but not from the droid.

'This building meets its needs for air and water. I scavenge food from across the city.'

Anna spun around in the direction of the voice. There was a man, a senior, maybe in his late seventies. His thinning hair was grey and white. A short beard hugged his tanned and crinkled face.

'I try to block all the openings. Some escape, but they always return,' he said. 'There's no need for the weapon.'

Anna kept the pistol aimed at him as he stepped forward.

'Stay where you are. Identify yourself,' she said.

The man stopped and smiled. 'Professor Dale.'

Anna glanced towards the motionless droid, then back at the professor. 'This is a dead zone. It's out of bounds.'

'Hmmm. Well, my apologies but I live here, with Humbro.' The professor gestured to the droid.

'How is it still functioning? There have been electromagnetic pulses for years to eradicate rogues,' said Anna.

'This place is lead-lined and deep,' the professor answered.

Anna side-eyed the robot. 'Your droid's not a rogue?'

'I helped develop the Syms. I've adjusted and modified Humbro for many years.'

The droid stepped forward, but halted as Anna twisted and pointed the pistol. She turned her aim back towards the professor.

He huffed. 'So, you've destroyed all the rogues.'

'Pretty much.'

'I wouldn't be so sure.'

'Any we've missed will soon be obliterated.' Anna half-turned and looked into the shadows. 'Who else is down here?'

'Just me and Humbro, and a few birds.'

'How many?' Anna asked.

'Oh, somewhere around ninety.'

'Well you, and they, are coming with me. The Earth is being quarantined.'

'Quarantined?' The professor laughed weakly. 'Well, so be it, but I'm staying and so are the birds.'

'I'm not requesting,' Anna gestured with her pistol.

'And what will you achieve? One more person on a space station. A couple more birds that will perish up there?' The professor shook his head.

'Every life we save is valuable; human or animal. Nothing will survive down here,' said Anna. 'The planet's dead, and it'll be dead for centuries.'

'Then I'll die here; the birds too. Except they won't.'

A sparrow landed next to the professor's feet and chirped. He breathed back a whisper.

'Of course they'll die,' Anna said. 'You think they'll survive in an underground hell?'

'And you think they'll survive on a space station?' the professor snapped back.

There was a long silence; the only sound the metronomic and distant echo of dripping water in a tunnel.

'The birds - they're the great survivors,' said the professor. 'They survived when the dinosaurs didn't, and they'll do it again.'

'How? You won't live forever. Then who'll look after them?'

'Humbro.'

Anna stepped forward and forcibly grabbed the professor's left arm. It was thin and weak. He fell as he tried to resist. The sparrow flew away.

'Time to go. This is for your own good.' Anna pulled the professor to his feet, surprised by the lightness of his body. 'We'll arrange for the birds to be removed.'

She hadn't noticed Humbro approaching until the droid twisted her free arm, causing the flare pistol to clatter to the ground. She released the professor and shoved the AI backwards. Crouching to snatch up the pistol, she aimed and fired. A cascade of sparks exploded from the droid's abdomen as a flare tore through a panel on its righthand side. It lurched forward and keeled over.

'No!' shouted the professor. Unsteadily, he tottered towards his fallen companion and stretched the droid on its back, waving a boney hand through the smoke rising from the AI's damaged central panel. 'You've destroyed his motor-control system, damn you. You've no idea what you've done. He's essential for the birds. He wasn't going to harm you, he wasn't a rogue.'

'I wasn't going to take the risk.'

'Well you should have.'

Anna grabbed the professor's arm again and dragged him away from the immobilized droid.

'Now you've no choice but to come with me.'

She thought only of her mission as she hauled the professor through the dank metro station and climbed the flights of stairs, ignoring his protests. She'd barely squeezed through the hole in the wall to reach the street outside when a voice crackled on the com-link attached to the lapel of her flight suit.

'Commander Anna, emergency alert. Exodus Shuttle 45 requests assistance,' said Sheean.

Anna released her grip and the professor dropped to his knees, his breathing turning from wheezing to a wretched rasp.

'What is it?' Anna asked Sheean.

'Message was disrupted by the gyro-storm above us. Rapid departure advised,' replied the onboard AI.

'Understood. I'm on my way.'

Anna turned to the professor, who was a crumpled ball on the ground, gasping for breath.

'I'll be back,' she said.

CHAPTER TWO

MIAMI

Anna rebooted into the exoskeleton suit and bounded to the scramjet. In moments, the craft soared above Manhattan and was consumed by a blanket of swirling dark clouds. Only when it emerged above the storm, where blue sky stretched from horizon to horizon, did the communication link crackle back to life.

'Exodus Shuttle 45 calling Gold Commander.' It was the captain of the shuttle.

'This is Gold Commander, go ahead Forty-Five,' Anna responded.

'Commander, we have a large vessel at sea closing in on our location.'

'What type of vessel?'

'A cruise ship, of sorts, Commander,' the captain said, his voice competing against crackling static.

'A drifting derelict?'

'No. It's under power and moving fast. We picked up a message relayed from it, requesting us to delay launch. It said there are survivors onboard.'

'Did you authenticate?' Anna asked.

'It's encrypted with an old fleet code. We've responded with current encryption, but without response.'

'How far is it from your location?'

'Four miles and closing. We're just north of Miami, near to the shoreline.'

'Understood,' said Anna. 'I thought you'd have departed by now, Forty-Five. What's your evacuation status?'

'We've another fifty to board. Final checks have commenced.'

'Speed things up. I'll deal with the vessel. Out.'

Anna instructed the onboard AI to set a course for the launch site.

'Auto-control engaged,' Sheean responded.

The scramjet pitched, turning towards the southwest. Punctuated by thudding shockwaves, the journey took only a few minutes. Anna recognized the panhandle coastline of Florida as the scramjet rocked gently, closing in on its destination and decelerating from Mach 10 to subsonic speed. No longer pressed hard into her seat, she felt her body lift against the buckles of the safety straps. Visible through the forward window were the tall buildings of downtown Miami, and beyond them the glistening waters of the North Atlantic, white streaked by parallel lines of waves.

'Sheean, give me control.' Anna placed her hands on the U-shaped joystick. A jolt rippled along her arms as the scramjet returned to manual control. She focused on the ocean and pinpointed the outline of a ship heading towards the coast. There was a dazzling burst of brightness as the sun's rays reflected off its windows. Nearing the cruise ship, the scramjet slowed.

'Sheean, identify object below.'

There was a short silence, then Sheean answered. 'No signals. No life readings. Unable to identify vessel.'

An image of the ship appeared on the dashboard screen.

'Let's take a look,' said Anna.

The scramjet banked, flying past at a tight angle.

'Vessel identified as Caribbean Dreamweaver,' Sheean announced.

'Details?'

The onboard AI said there was no record of the cruise ship returning to sea after berthing five years ago in New Jersey.

The scramjet gently hovered above the bow of the Caribbean Dreamweaver, allowing Anna to peer into its deserted control bridge. Turning the scramjet to the starboard side, she studied the empty passenger decks. It was a ghost ship, traveling at maximum speed towards the coastline; specifically towards the location of Exodus Shuttle 45.

Anna asked for another full scan of the ship. Sheean reported it was negative for life forms, AIs and droids.

'Something must be guiding it. I'm going to take a closer look,' said Anna. 'Sheean, resume control. Land on rear deck. There's something there that doesn't look right.'

She had spotted a metal shipping container wedged into the swimming pool on the sundeck. Under automated control, the scramjet maneuvered to the left of the pool and landed vertically on the deck.

'How's the air outside?' Anna asked as she unbuckled from the pilot seat.

'Air quality poor. Level five. High radioactivity in vicinity.'

Anna climbed into her exoskeleton suit, slotting the helmet into its rigid collar rim. She strapped the pistol holster to her right thigh and took a deep breath of the suit's regulated air supply. Taking the pistol from the holster, she pointed it straight ahead as the scramjet's hatch door opened. Outside, she paused at the end of the entry ramp, turning slowly one way and then another.

'Sheean, close and seal scramjet. Only open at my command.'

She stepped off the ramp and approached the rusting shipping container in the drained swimming pool. From a pouch in her suit she pulled out a small baton-shaped monitor. The monitoring device buzzed to life, emitting a red and blue pulse from two diode lights. She waved it towards the metal container, then quickly stepped backwards.

'Critical radioactivity. Sheean, find origin of container. I'm heading for the bridge.'

Deserted interior gangways, long and nondescript, were illuminated by flickering emergency lighting and punctuated by uniformly spaced cabin doors. Some were open, offering snatched glimpses of neat suites within; bare, faded and shorn of warmth.

A shorter hallway emerged into a large dining area. Dust-covered tables and chairs stretched from wall to wall. Anna skirted along the fringe of the room, stopping at the last table. Unlike the others it had not been cleared. Near the center were two wine glasses and a half empty bottle of wine. She lowered her pistol and leaned forward, using a finger to wipe a layer of dust from the label on the bottle to reveal the name of a decade-old Chardonnay.

'Those were the days,' she said softly, triggering in her mind an image of distant days as she imagined the dining hall alive with passengers, echoing with ripples of laughter and idle vacation chatter. She felt a pang of longing and regret. Snapping back to the moment, her eyes swept across the room one last time before she resumed her walk towards the front of the ship.

The door to the control bridge was locked. She aimed at it and fired the pistol. There was a sharp crack and a flare exploded against the door. She stepped forward and kicked it open, swinging her pistol in all directions as she entered the control room. It was deserted. The only noise was her own breathing, fast and shallow, and the distant hum of the ship's turbines.

'Sheean, any change in readings?' she asked, speaking into the helmet's com-link while examining a glowing bank of lights and dials on the central control console.

'Negative. No life onboard, other than you.'

'Drones, droids?'

'Negative.'

Through the large aft windows, the coastline of Florida and the tallest buildings of Miami were visible. The city's boundaries were marked by the shattered remains of the immense glass and steel dome that had once protected it. Almost every city across the developed world had been encased in such domes, but the protection they offered against the collapsing climate was not enough. Domes that had not all ready been compromised by nature's rampant destructive forces had been destroyed in the wars. A few miles north of the pitiful shards of Miami's dome, the gleaming white fuselage of Exodus Shuttle 45 pointed skyward. The Caribbean Dreamweaver was sailing directly towards it.

Anna holstered her pistol and with both gloved hands attempted to engage the console controls. There was no response. She flicked more switches and swiped her fingers across the master screen; still nothing. Then something caught her attention. A small brown box affixed to the console. It was smooth on all sides, devoid of markings or controls. She placed a hand around it and tugged, but the box held fast even against the exoskeleton suit's augmented power.

'Are you seeing this, Sheean?' she asked, knowing the AI monitored everything through the cameras that were attached to her suit.

'Affirmative. Device appears to have an imperfection on its right side.'

Anna leant forward. 'I don't see anything. Are you sure?'

'Affirmative, midway across and on the lower half.'

'I'm still not seeing anything. I need to remove my gloves. Advise, Sheean.'

The answer was unequivocal. Toxic chemical pollution in the air made it unsafe to breathe, and radiation levels were dangerously elevated. Sheean advised her to remain fully in the exoskeleton suit. Anna raised her head and looked through the windows of the bridge room at the approaching coastline.

'I'll take the risk,' she said, unclipping the thick gloves from her suit and putting them into a side pocket. Her bare fingertips slid across the side of the mystery box.

'Found it.'

She peered closely at the spot where the texture of the box was almost imperceivably altered. She unclipped a pocket on her suit and pulled out a short, serrated hunting knife and scraped it against the box. It had no impact. She pushed harder with rapid backward and forward motions. This time flakes of material peeled away, scattering onto the console. A small electronic data input socket emerged. She stopped scraping.

'Sheean, I'm going to connect to the device. Tell me what you find.'

Anna took a computer tablet from another pouch on her suit and unhooked its connector cable, stretching it until she could insert it into the socket on the box. The tablet's screen lit up with flashing streams of computer coding.

'Device is automated guidance control piloting the ship,' reported Sheean.

'Can you override?'

'Negative. Superior and unorthodox coding has loaded tamper alerts.'

'Loaded tamper alerts? Explain.' Anna's eyes darted upwards to the windows and the approaching coastline.

'Tampering with the programmed operation of the device will trigger immediate destruction of the ship,' said Sheean.

'What's the programmed destination?'

'Device is locked-on to coordinates of Exodus Shuttle 45. It is instructed to simultaneously activate explosives onboard the ship when it is within one mile of target,' said Sheean.

'How far are we from the shuttle?'

'Two-point-one miles. Ship will enter one mile radius in approximately four minutes.'

Anna's blood chilled. It had taken ten minutes to walk to the bridge room.

'Sheean, connect me to Exodus Shuttle 45.'

The link was activated.

'This is Gold Commander to Exodus Shuttle 45. Urgent,' she said.

'Exodus Shuttle 45. Yes, commander?' the shuttle captain replied through crackling static.

'Launch immediately,' Anna ordered. She heard an exchange of voices in the background, but through the static could not decipher their words. Then the captain returned.

'We can't launch, we need time to load the final passengers. Another fifteen minutes at least,' he said.

'Captain, you have three minutes to launch or no-one gets out. Close bulkhead and go.'

'There are people on the gangplank,' the captain protested.

'They're too late. Seal doors and launch. That's an order. Over.'

Anna stifled a gag reflex in her throat as she imagined the terror and chaos outside the exodus shuttle.

'Sheean, bring the scramjet level with the bridge and lower tethering cable.'

The AI acknowledged the request.

'Where did the ship commence its journey?' Anna asked. A set of coordinates was projected onto the inside of her visor.

'32N, 64W,' Anna read aloud. 'That's the middle of the ocean.'

'Coordinates are islands of Bermuda,' corrected Sheean. 'Scramjet now starboard. Tethering cable lowered.'

Anna returned the tablet to the pouch on her suit. At the exterior door of the bridge room she pressed down on a hinged steel bar. The door opened, but with barely enough clearance for her to squeeze through wearing the exoskeleton suit. The scramjet hovered twenty feet above. With her ungloved hands she grabbed the dangling cable, swinging a foot upwards to step on to a heavy metal hook at the end.

'Sheean, return to the rear deck and lower me onto the container.'

The scramjet lifted vertically and reversed the length of the ship until it hovered above the rear deck.

Anna was lowered onto the roof of the metal shipping container. She clipped the tethering cable's hook to a holding point at one corner.

'Lift container and bring me underside. Open hatch.'

When enough of the cable had been retracted, she hauled herself through the hatch in the scramjet's undercarriage. Beneath her, the metal container swayed on the end of the tethering cable. The hatch clanked shut and Anna removed her helmet.

'Sheean, set course for Bermuda. Best speed.'

There was a buzz on the com-link.

'Exodus Shuttle 45 launching. Commander, we've left behind more than thirty...'

'I know, captain,' Anna interrupted. 'There was no alternative. Make contact with Artemis Control when you're clear of the stratospheric dead zone. Over.'

Anna stepped from the cumbersome confines of the exoskeleton suit. She reached the cockpit and strapped in as the scramjet pierced a supersonic bow wave. The dashboard screen recorded Mach 1, with the speed accelerating rapidly.

'There's a high probability container contains explosive ordinance linked to ship's primed controls,' said Sheean.

'Hopefully it's the only radioactive material on the ship. How long before it reaches trigger zone?' asked Anna.

'Forty-two seconds.'

The scramjet rocked as it burst through a second sonic shockwave.

'Jettison tethering cable at 20 seconds, and then maximum acceleration,' said Anna, silently counting the seconds. A mechanical thump reverberated through the scramjet.

'Cable release malfunction,' reported Sheean.

'What!' Anna unbuckled and staggered to the rear cabin. She lurched forward, slamming both hands against a lever adjacent to the hatch door. It didn't move. Her knuckles trembled white as she pushed again, this time with her legs braced against the bulkhead. The lever jumped an inch, then another. She screamed and pushed harder, toppling forward as the lever relented and jettisoned the cable.

Prostrate on the cabin floor, sweat trickling from her forehead, she gulped for air. There was a deafening explosion. She was lifted upwards, losing her grip on the lever and slamming against the cabin's ceiling. Pitched into an uncontrolled somersault, she cracked her head against the floor and lost consciousness.

CHAPTER THREE

BERMUDA

Opening one eye, Anna saw red. Wiping the blood away, she squinted. She was on her back, sprawled awkwardly on the floor. There was an electrifying jolt of pain as she attempted to open her left eye. Clam-like swollen skin, tender to the touch, filled the socket. The scramjet was juddering and swaying, and the interior lighting was unusually subdued and minimal. Bruised and battered, Anna stumbled twice before reaching and slumping into the pilot seat. Outside the cockpit window she saw the ocean stretching away to a hazy horizon.

'Sheean, damage report.'

'Main power drive inoperative; auxiliary power only. Cruising speed, 0.3 Mach. Altitude 9,000 feet and declining. Communication module destroyed. External scanning systems undetected, presumed lost.'

'What happened to main drive?' Anna wiped a trickle of fresh blood from her open right eye.

'Catastrophic external damage to power unit caused by explosion.'

'The container?'

'Affirmative. Nuclear air blast was within radius of six miles.'

'A dirty bomb,' Anna concluded.

'Energy release suggests tactical nuclear device was triggered,' Sheean confirmed.

Anna placed a hand on the flight console touchscreen, activating a map image. There was a small landmass fifty-five miles northeast.

'Sheean, identify island.'

'Archipelago of Bermuda,' Sheean replied.

Anna glanced at the telemetry. The scramjet had slowed to 0.25 Mach and its altitude had dropped to 7,500 feet.

'Can we reach it?' she asked.

'Negative. At current velocity ocean landing will occur three miles from south coast of main island.'

Anna swiveled to her right, stood up and took five unsteady steps to the rear cabin. 'Would it help if we reduced weight? Is there anything that can be ejected?'

'Mechanical stores and expired auxiliary fuel cells can be released,' said Sheean.

'Do it.'

Anna returned to the cockpit. From the pilot's seat she stared out at the ocean. There was a metallic clank as the ballast was released.

'How much difference does it make?'

'Landing will now occur half-a-mile from island,' said Sheean.

It wasn't enough. As the speed and altitude readings fell, Anna slapped the armrests. Then she pictured a childhood image. She was playing by a pond. The sun's bright reflection danced between the spindly shadows of a willow tree's branches, the lowest dipping towards the pond but not reaching its refreshing water. Beyond the willow were voices; her parents, and the high-pitched squeals of other youngsters. She gathered up saucer-shaped stones at the pond's edge, holding them in one small palm and rubbing her other hand across their smooth, cool surface. From her squat position she half-stood, then twisted with her right elbow tucked against her stomach and sent one of the stones spinning towards the water. It skimmed the surface, hopping five times and leaving a string of expanding circular ripples in its wake before sinking near the center.

'Five!' the young Anna declared.

'Well done,' her mother acknowledged from beyond the willow.

The youngster smiled and resumed her half-crouched position and skimmed another stone. It hopped four times.

The image faded and Anna was once again aware of the ocean through the scramjet's window. She saw a shape on the horizon - Bermuda - and grabbed the control joystick to lower the ship. Her good eye focused on the undulating contours of the island.

'Is there a beach?' she asked.

'A half-mile expanse of sand in a sheltered bay is directly ahead,' replied Sheean.

Anna steadied the scramjet, lowering its altitude until the hypnotic, rippled seascape of the ocean was sixty feet below.

'Sheean, what is the optimum speed to achieve bounce on ocean surface?'

'Bounce from shallow glide path should be possible above forty-five miles per hour. Danger of stalling at slower speed.'

A film of sweat coated Anna's palms as she tightened her grip on the controls and lowered the scramjet to within ten feet of the ocean. Bermuda was closer, and the shapes of individual palms, cedars and casuarina trees could now be discerned. Pastel colored houses and cottages, their white roofs gleaming in the sunlight, were scattered across the hillsides.

The shoreline appeared a long way ahead. The scramjet's speed was now fifty miles per hour and falling. Anna knew the danger of hesitating even for a few seconds.

'Let's go,' she said, pushing against the joystick. The craft's underbelly thudded against the waves then bounced back into the air, fizzing forward. Anna braced for the next jolt as the scramjet skimmed the ocean again and flicked back up.

'Two.' She counted the hops. The hum of the engine was extinguished; all fuel used. Momentum alone now carried the craft. Forward speed was twenty miles per hour; each contact with the ocean dragged that number down.

'Three.' She counted another thud. 'One more, one more.' She glimpsed the speed indicator showing seven miles per hour as her vision was blurred by another bone-rattling thud. There was barely any upward lift before a final shuddering bang as the scramjet carved through the shallow water, the dregs of momentum forcing it onto the beach and into higher dunes. When it became stationary, hydraulics hissed as they battled to deploy the landing legs, two to the rear and one below the cockpit. The scramjet pitched to one side, then straightened as it was lifted seven feet higher by the hydraulic props. The hissing subsided and the only noise was the steady beat of waves folding onto the beach. Anna unstrapped and contemplated the view outside where smooth, untrammeled sand stretched away in all directions.

'Sheean, can you give me an outside air reading?'

'Negative. All external systems inoperable,' said Sheean, reiterating that all communication and telemetry modules had been destroyed by the earlier explosion.

The sand dunes that had halted the scramjet's sliding crash were topped by spindly course grass and succulent plants adapted to semi-tropical heat. Beyond them towered a steeper slope with bushes and thinly foliaged trees. Anna's gaze was drawn to the majestic fronds of mature palms at its summit.

'What do we have on record about this place?' she asked.

'Island was evacuated eight months ago. City of Hamilton's dome shell was breached by rogue AIs in assault prior to evacuation,' said Sheean.

'AIs,' said Anna. 'They must still be here. This is where that cruise ship set sail. Any information on the evacuation? Was it successful?'

'One exodus shuttle was destroyed, another departed with remaining population. Unverified account of runners within damaged city before departure of shuttle.'

'Runners.' Anna's voice was a mix of hope and foreboding. Runners was a term used to describe fugitives opposed to the mandatory evacuation who had evaded the authorities. On previous sorties she had rounded up small groups of runaways, all of them suffering terminal health conditions after weeks of exposure to the toxic conditions.

'Could they have survived for eight months? What have the outside conditions been?' she asked.

Sheean was unable to confirm atmospheric status beyond the departure report of the sole successful shuttle. Anna rested her hands against the rim of the window. She'd reached the safety of land, but didn't know if there was anyone still on the island, or even if its atmosphere was livable. She was stuck on a dying planet unable to contact Alpha rendezvous or Artemis Control. Worse, she had an intimate knowledge of the devastating timeline now playing out.

'How long until global planetary quarantine?' she asked.

'Three days, eight hours and twelve minutes.'

Anna shuddered. 'How far is the city?'

'Overland route is seven miles. There is a direct route of two-and-a-half miles across sheltered waters,' Sheean answered.

'That's too far wearing the exoskeleton. I'll go like this.'

'Not advised,' said Sheean.

Anna ignored the warning. A few minutes later, wearing a flight suit with a light backpack, and the flare pistol strapped to her thigh, she opened the hatch door and was met with a blast of hot, humid air. She paused at the end of the ramp, adjusting her good eye to the intensity of the sun. Pristine sand, smooth and graduating from bleached white to a pinkish hue, stretched into the distance. The digital pad she held indicated the air quality was degraded but breathable. The radiation level was elevated, but also within an acceptable range. The soft sand yielded as she stepped away from the craft. Turning, she examined two large holes that had been ripped in the scramjet's fuselage, one contained the charred remains of the telemetry and communications unit. At the rear, only one of the four engine nozzle jets was intact. The damage appeared beyond repair.

'Sheean, close door and seal scramjet. Open only at my command.'

The ramp retracted and the hatch closed. With the metronomic sound of lapping waves to her right, Anna lifted her head to the trees and the sky. There was no movement other than the breezy swaying of branches. She reached the edge of the dunes at the foot of a steep sand-covered hill and snapped off a branch from a bush. Its crisp leaves were fading to a toxic shock brown. She retraced her steps to the scramjet, then swept the branch against the sand to obliterate her footprints as she backed up once more to the edge of the dunes. Her trail had vanished. It was a drill from her formative training years. Would it fool a rogue AI, or anyone else who might be out there? She had her doubts.

Climbing the sandy hinterland she dodged the jagged, sword-shaped leaves of Spanish bayonets. Nearing the summit, at the steepest part of the climb, she slipped on loose sand and grabbed at prickly grass and an exposed tree root to save herself.

Finally, standing on the ridge of the hill, she wiped sweat from her forehead and looked back at the beach. In the sandy landscape the scramjet appeared small. The only noise was her breathing and an almost imperceivable whispering breeze threading through the needles of the casuarinas. She consulted the computer oracle pad, bringing up a map showing routes to Hamilton, the island's small central city. The land option was eastwards, but she headed north for the far shorter land and sea combination.

For an hour the terrain was undulating, passing along narrow streets shorn of sidewalks, bordered by empty homes painted mostly in pastel shades of pink, blue, and green. Outside a red-colored house she stopped and unzipped a pocket on her backpack to take out a flask of water. She drank copiously and eyed the inviting shade of the house's veranda. Six wooden steps took her to the front door.

Dumping her backpack next to a wooden chair on the veranda, she peered through a grimy window into a dimly lit front room. A layer of dust coated the furniture inside, and there was evidence the previous occupants had left in a hurry; papers and possessions were scattered and an abandoned half-filled packing case rested in a corner. She stepped back and let herself collapse into the slatted wooden chair. The relief was all consuming. She closed her eyes and rested her head against the chair back.

How long she had been asleep she was not sure, but she awoke with a start, almost falling from the chair. The breeze had become a strong and portentous wind. Wooden shutters on a house opposite rattled. Was it the wind? She froze and looked intently at the rocking shutters. She pulled the oracle pad from a pocket and held it at arm's length, performing a sweeping 180-degree arc. It detected no lifeforms within range and no electronic radiation that would indicate AI activity. She touched the screen, bringing up a display that showed the air quality had deteriorated and the radiation count had risen to a level barely within the safe zone. Grabbing her backpack she jumped up and jogged down the steps from the veranda, resuming her walk northwards at a quicker pace, hoping the dome shell of the city would be intact enough to provide shelter from the failing atmospheric conditions.

At the end of the street she caught sight of a large expanse of water. It was a mile wide. On the far side were silhouettes of tall buildings enclosed by a steel and glass dome - the city of Hamilton. Straining her good eye, she searched for signs of damage to the dome, but saw none. She checked her route; there was a gradual slope ahead leading to the waterside, a dock and a few small boats. Quickening her pace, she passed along more streets that were filled with white-roofed houses. She stopped three times to scan for life or AIs. The readings were negative.

The total silence of her surroundings was unsettling. It had been this way at all previous landings on her mission searching for stragglers, fugitives and any other life. But she had never grown accustomed to the absence of sound. No dogs barked, no bees buzzed, no birds chirped. Just an aural void. She'd always had a way to reach out to others through her com-link, or to contact Sheean in the scramjet. Now she could do neither. She continued walking, stopping only momentarily whenever she thought she'd heard something. Each time there was nothing. As the wind strengthened, she was thankful to be sheltered by the close-packed houses and the lee of the high ground that now separated her from the beach.

Reaching lower ground, trees and houses blocked the view of the domed city and the inner harbor, but she had a good sense of direction and followed a small winding road to reach the dock at the waterside. Small fishing and pleasure boats were dotted around the shore, and there was a compact passenger ferry at the end of a short pier. However, the boats were afloat at unnatural angles; their hulls damaged, cracked or holed near the waterline.

She conducted a fruitless search for a boat that was unscathed before noticing a shed on the far side of a second pier. Prizing out a rusty pin that held the shed's double doors closed, she peered inside and saw a jet-ski resting on a rubber mat. She pulled it out and dragged it across the wooden pier to a ramp that dipped into the water.

The wind strengthened, tugging at the landscape, but it was not responsible for a chill that swept across Anna. She froze and listened. Everything seemed as deserted as it had been, yet she sensed she was no longer alone.

CHAPTER FOUR

HAMILTON

Anna pulled out the oracle device and swept it around in a full arc. There were no life readings. She clicked it off and shook her head, then refocused on the jet-ski controls. A key was tied to one handgrip. Inserting it into the ignition slot, she gave it a twist. The engine spluttered and caught at the third attempt, revving to life. She pushed the water craft down the ramp into the knee-deep shallows, swinging herself onto the seat and gripping the handlebars to send it roaring into the harbor. Threading past small islands and islets, she headed for the city dome of Hamilton on the far side. A westerly wind raked through the expanse of the Great Sound as dark clouds devoured the blue sky.

It took fifteen minutes to reach the harbor-side at the city. Berthing next to a set of steps, she found an old rope dangling from the dockside and tied the jet-ski to the harbor wall. Multi-story buildings were visible through the glass and steel dome that encased the city; their exteriors decorated in a mixture of pastel colors similar to the houses and cottages on the other side of the harbor. She skirted around the edge of the dome, stopping to take scanner readings that continued to read negative for life.

At ground level the dome had suffered superficial damage and small breaks, but was mostly intact. Anna found a gaping entrance to the dome's sanctuary. It was nine feet wide and a similar height. The jagged edges indicated the breach had been caused by force, either through entry or exit. Stepping through the gap, she found herself in a world of silent city streets beneath the soaring cathedral-like dome.

Daylight was fading. She quickened her pace as she searched. Everything indicated there had been an orderly evacuation. Inside an office building she tried an elevator. There was no power. Climbing eight flights of stairs she reached the top and burst though an access door onto a flat roof that afforded views across the city. The dome creaked as the wind pushed against it, yet within its protective shield all was calm. She absorbed the silence as she leant against a steel rail to peer at the streets below, where shadows had grown in the gloom of the approaching storm.

She consulted the oracle pad. The air quality remained poor, verging into the red zone. Radiation and toxicity levels had fallen due to the protection of the dome. She felt a shiver; it was the same uneasy sensation she'd felt at the dockside. She swiped a finger across the oracle pad screen, then pointed it in the direction of the city's center. It bleeped. It had detected an electronically-controlled movement. Was it a search droid or an AI? Her heart skipped. She withdrew from the edge as she memorized as much of the city layout as she could, then retraced her steps down the staircase and back into the unlit streets.

At the first street corner she stopped and checked the oracle pad. There was no signal. A sudden loud metallic bang made her jump and point the device in its direction. The reading was negative. Perhaps it was a heavy door swinging shut, she thought. The only wind within the dome was at its damaged edges.

Facing the direction of the noise, she backed away. After five steps there was a deep whining, animalistic sound from behind. She whirled around, pointing the oracle pad towards the deep shadows. Nothing. Then there was another metallic bang, closer and louder. She put the pad away, unclipped her pistol and backed into a store entrance. The store's main door was locked. She pushed against it, then crouched and stuck her head out from the doorway to peer along the street.

There was a blur of movement in front of her, then a heavy blow against her left temple. She fell hard and awkwardly against the sidewalk, dropping the pistol as she was kicked in her right side. Winded, she struggled to breathe and tried to roll away. She glimpsed a flash of metal and light, and a humanoid shape; its movements stilted and mechanical. A hand reached down, grabbing the collar of her flight suit and pulling her upwards. Now face-to-face with her assailant she stared at its human-like features and saw blankness in its glowing red eyes. It was an AI, a Sym-54 droid.

'Who are you?' Anna croaked, her voice fading as she struggled to breathe, her feet dangling above the sidewalk as the AI held her tightly. The droid's head turned quickly to one side, momentarily distracted. It flung her in the same direction. Anna's head cracked against the ground. The droid stepped forward and crushed the discarded pistol. It bent over and grabbed Anna by the midriff, this time pushing a metallic hand into the front pouch of her flight suit, extracting the oracle pad and hurling it to the opposite side of the street, where it shattered against a wall.

The droid brutally lifted Anna and took aim at the same wall. She screamed. The droid's face was emotionless, then it froze and turned from the wall. Its red eyes peered into the darkness in the direction of a whining noise. It was the same noise Anna had heard moments earlier. Now it sounded closer. She gasped for breath and mouthed a protest, but was robbed of her voice by exhaustion and fear. Holding her in one hand, the droid took slow, steady steps. When it reached the street corner, Anna trained her open eye on the darkness and tried to spot the source of the whining, which was now an echoing howl. Then she saw it - a human figure pointing a pistol.

There was a flash of light, a loud retort. A bullet whistled past and struck the AI. The droid staggered backwards, losing its grip on Anna. She landed in an ungainly heap and instinctively flattened herself against the road to avoid a volley of gunfire. Twisting, she saw the AI flounder in the hail of bullets. It lost its footing and keeled over, landing with a sickening thud. There was a smell of burning wires, blown electronics and gunshot residue. Wisps of smoke rose from holes in the droid's motionless body.

'You,' a voice called out. Anna rolled over and looked up. It was a man. His dark-toned facial features were obscured in the shadows of a hood. Her good eye fixed on the gun he pointed.

'Who are you,' he asked.

'I'm...I'm not an AI.'

'I can see that.' His eyes flicked to Anna's right arm. She followed his gaze and saw a large patch of her white flight suit was now red, soaked in blood at the elbow and forearm.

'One last time, who are you?' the man asked, menacingly standing over her.

'I'm Gold Commander for Project Exodus. I'm overseeing the final evacuation.' Anna tried to sit up. Her throat felt dry, she coughed to clear it. The man's eyes shifted to examine the badges on her flight-suit.

'American?' he asked.

'Yes.'

The gun was withdrawn and stowed out of sight inside his jacket. He reached down, grabbing Anna by one hand and pulling her onto her feet.

'What happened to your eye?'

'An accident,' Anna replied, touching the swollen left socket.

'Isn't the exodus complete yet?'

'Almost.' Anna brushed her suit and examined her blood-stained right elbow. 'You shouldn't be here,' she added. 'This island was cleared.'

'Not so much,' the man laughed, then abruptly stopped and looked around, listening intently. 'We'd better go. The AIs rarely travel alone. They'll soon be here to check on this unit.'

'There are more?'

'Oh yeah.' The man walked back to the corner and turned. 'This way. You got any friends?'

'Not in here,' Anna answered, unsure whether she could trust him.

'Hmmm. Outside the city?'

'I'd rather not say.'

The man twirled around and aggressively grabbed Anna's flight suit at the same spot on the collar where she had been gripped by the AI.

'Listen,' he said. 'If there are others you better tell me if you want them to survive. Five seconds, four, three, two...'

'No. Only me.'

The man released his grip.

'There's a safe place at the edge of the city, that's where we'll go tonight,' he said, his anger receding. 'Follow me and don't deviate, this place is booby-trapped. And no talking.'

Anna noticed he had a slight limp. She guessed he was in his fifties. Through the darkness they took a winding route. Some of the twists occurred in the middle of a street; right-angle turns for no obvious reason, ducking down alleys. Every few minutes the man stopped and observed the surroundings, turning to check Anna was staying close. The only sound was their footsteps and the hum and creak of the wind against the dome.

They diverted into a low profile building. The man pulled out a flashlight to guide the way along unlit corridors until they encountered a steel door. He twisted a handle and the door slowly opened. When the gap was wide enough he squeezed through and beckoned Anna. The heavy door was pushed closed behind them, clanking against its frame before a thick steel bar was lowered in place to secure it.

'That should hold,' the man said. They continued the trek through the darkness. The flashlight's beam picked out a staircase. They descended four flights and reached a small open space, where there was another steel door, this time ajar. Once through it, the man repeated what he had done previously, sealing it closed with a metal bar. He shone the torchlight across a wall to locate a control box, where he flicked two switches. Ceiling lights were energized, revealing the interior of a large room. It was barren except for a dining table with two chairs, a couple of camp beds with bedding, and a kitchenette with a sink, countertop electric stove and microwave oven. Scattered on the floor were a few boxes of packaged food.

'The AIs destroyed most of the city's solar arrays, but there are a few still hidden that provide power,' explained the man. 'Here's something for you.'

He placed a bandage reel and a box of plasters on the table. Anna took them and rolled up the bloodied sleeve of her flight suit. The grazed skin was still weeping. She placed a large plaster over the injury.

'I'll make something to eat,' the man said. He started preparing a meal using dried vegetables and canned produce. 'You got a name, other than Gold Commander?'

'Anna. And you?'

He was Charlie, aged 72, and a native Bermudian.

'You're a runner,' Anna stated.

'Runner? Not me. Never run in my life.'

'No, a runner, a fugitive.'

Charlie turned. 'Is that what you call us? Runners?'

'You ran from the evacuation; you're a runner.'

'And you and the rest ran from the AIs. So you're the runner.' There was a hint of anger in his voice.

'We're saving mankind.' Anna said. She sat down on a chair beside the table. 'We're starting again, not hiding away in a hole waiting for the inevitable.'

'The inevitable, and what's that?'

'Extinction.'

At the kitchenette counter Charlie stirred a pot on the small stove, his back to Anna. 'So you say,' he said.

'So I know. Anyone with an ounce of intelligence can see what's happening.'

'Hey, stop running your mouth, 'cause you know I'll give it right back,' Charlie snapped, turning to stare at her.

The conversation ceased. Anna concentrated on wrapping a thin cloth bandage over the plaster on her arm, then rolled the blood-covered sleeve back down. She thought about the AI that had attacked her, and the other AIs that had gone rogue towards the end of the wars that had annihilated most of the world's population. The AIs took it upon themselves to hunt down all survivors, using whatever means to sabotage the planetary evacuation. They were determined that humans should not spread their destruction beyond the Earth. The evacuation was primarily to flee the poisoned world, but also to escape from the marauding AIs.

Anna's train of thought ended when Charlie declared the food was ready. He dished it onto two plates and carried them to the table.

'The others, will I meet them?' Anna asked.

'What others?'

'The other runners.'

Charlie's eyes avoided Anna's. There was an uncomfortable silence until he finally spoke, changing the subject.

'Your ship, where is it?'

'On a beach. It barely reached the shore.'

'How so?'

'There was an explosion. I limped here with what power remained and ditched.'

'Can it be repaired?' Charlie had finished his food and pushed his plate to one side.

'No, it lost its communication and monitoring systems and three engines.'

'Huh. How do I know you're not lying?'

'You don't, but it's the truth.' There was still food on her plate, but Anna placed her cutlery together and slid it away.

'Then you're stuck here,' Charlie said, carrying the plates to the sink.

'Unless I find a way to contact Artemis Control. What technology is still operational? Is there a com-center?'

Charlie laughed. 'You think the AIs would allow that? No. Every piece of useful equipment and technology they've gathered for themselves, or destroyed. They want us gone, all of us, and anything that sustains us.'

Anna nodded.

'And even if there was a way to communicate or get off this island. What would you do?' Charlie added, scrubbing the plates.

'Continue my mission.' Anna was blunt. 'The evacuation orders are mandatory. No one is to be left behind.'

'I know. One of your colleagues was here. Dressed like you. Same mission, same attitude.'

'What happened to them?'

Charlie ignored the question and finished cleaning the plates.

'And me?' he finally asked. 'What would you do about me and the others. Round us up, take us back?'

'That's my mission...' Anna paused. 'Was my mission. But this is hypothetical. I'm stuck here like you and the others.'

'Just so I know.' Charlie walked to one of the camp beds against the far wall. 'It's late and we have an early start tomorrow. We should get some sleep.'

Anna said nothing, but made her way to the camp bed in the opposite corner. She laid down and closed her eyes. There was a click and the room was plunged into darkness.

* * *

When Anna awoke the room light was on. She checked her watch, she'd slept for seven hours. Groggily she sat up, swinging her feet onto the floor beside the bed. She now had vision in both her right eye and through the chink of an opening in the still swollen left one.

Charlie was at the kitchenette preparing breakfast. 'Good morning,' he said, half turning from a small pot he was stirring on the stove. 'There's a bathroom down the corridor on the right. Take the torch.'

Anna collected the flashlight from the table and walked to the door, which was no longer sealed shut. When she returned from the bathroom she joined Charlie at the table. Breakfast was oatmeal porridge.

Unbid, Charlie began to describe his life. Before the wars he'd worked as a taxi driver. It gave him a comfortable income, but there were fallow times when tourist numbers waned and hardships gripped the island. He recounted how the wars and climate destruction had left most of Bermuda's people on the brink of ruin. He became agitated when he talked about 'the before times', pausing to dampen his anger.

Anna spoke to re-engage him. 'The evacuation. Tell me what happened.'

Charlie had finished his porridge.

'It was going well,' he said. 'The population was about two thousand. We'd lost sixty thousand to radiation, the wars, the hunger. Things had been breaking down for a long time. We knew that the AIs could no longer be trusted; we deactivated as many as we could, but not enough. They took their revenge.'

'How?' Anna lent forward.

'Any way and every way. Our secured water supplies were poisoned. Food warehouses were burnt to the ground. Equipment malfunctioned.' Charlie looked at the wall, then back at Anna. 'The biggest incident was the gas and oil terminal. The inferno destroyed the whole of St George, not only the town - everything; the whole parish.'

Anna used the silence that followed to observe Charlie. His once brown hair had aged to almost pure white. Some of the skin on his forehead showed damage from decades under intense sunshine. His hands, although wrinkled, were thick and strong.

'Are you from St George?' she asked.

Charlie nodded and brought his attention back to the table. 'The attacks began,' he said. 'They seized weapons from the Regiment barracks and used them against the survivors. They sabotaged the city's dome. There was almost no-one left to evacuate by the time a shuttle arrived.'

'How many got away?'

'Two hundred, maybe less. A few of us stayed.'

'Why?'

'This is our home,' Charlie became animated. 'We've lived here all our lives and we didn't want to leave. We'd found ways to get at the AIs. We thought we could eradicate them.'

'But the evacuation orders were mandatory. No one was to be left behind.'

Charlie nodded. There was a long silence.

'What happened to my colleague?' Anna asked. 'The one you spoke of last night.'

Charlie sighed. 'Maybe it would have all been different if we hadn't run. The AIs knew what was happening and they attacked those preparing for the evacuation. We had decided we'd stay and refused to comply with the evacuation. We ran.'

'How many of you?'

'Fifteen, sixteen. We had places that were safe and hidden from both sides. The shuttle left, but your colleague stayed and came after us. The AIs got him before he got us.'

Anna put down her spoon.

'I'm sorry,' Charlie said, taking his bowl to the kitchenette and rinsing it out.

'The others. Will I meet them?' Anna asked.

'We'll see.' Charlie glanced at his watch. 'We need to move as soon as the sun rises, that'll make things easier. The AIs won't be expecting activity so early.'

The next hour was spent packing and tidying. Charlie filled two rucksacks with items. The room was left neat, ready for its next visitors. Who would they be, Anna enquired.

'Me. Alone,' Charlie replied. 'The others stay in the shelter as much as possible. I don't mind being out, being exposed. I'm older, my time is limited, but I'm still strong.'

When satisfied with the orderly appearance of the room, they left. Charlie locked the door and used the flashlight to guide the way back through the building and up to street level.

Outside, the first rays of daylight bathed the tips of the tallest buildings and bounced off the dome's steel lattice framework. Beyond the glass bubble a blue sky was streaked by wispy white clouds. The wind that had howled the previous evening was gone.

They walked swiftly. Charlie abruptly stopped at regular intervals, listening for any noise. They reached a supermarket and he led the way to the rear and climbed onto a dusty docking bay, grabbing a chain pulley that caused a steel roller shutter door to lift. Inside the dim space was a small truck.

'This is our chariot out of here.' Charlie opened the driver side door. 'I use it to haul food and supplies.'

The rear of the truck had been filled with items taken from the supermarket shelves and storerooms. It was mostly dry food, along with other supplies gathered from elsewhere in the city. Charlie explained how the loaded truck was driven across the island and hidden at a spot where it could be retrieved for the next excursion to the city. So far, the AIs had not intercepted it, although there had been an attempt previously, when he had feinted a crash and buried himself in thick undergrowth to escape from two AIs.

As its engine came to life the truck shuddered. Once outside Charlie closed the shutter door. Using his knowledge of the city, he navigated the truck to the edge of the dome and through an opening. They followed an undulating, windy road. Cottages were dotted along it, each painted a pastel shade. Anna asked about their ubiquitous pitched white roofs. Charlie explained that the island had no freshwater rivers or lakes, and often suffered long dry spells. Preserving rainwater allowed the islanders to survive and prosper, and the concept had been incorporated in the design of buildings since the 1600s when Bermuda was first settled.

'The white limestone roof tiles keep the rainwater clean,' Charlie said. 'It runs down the stepped tiles into pipes and underground storage, then it's drawn on when required.

'Is that what you and the others do?' Anna asked.

Charlie kept his eye on the road and nodded. 'We have a large catchment that does the same thing. Although I wonder about the water quality now.'

The sun cleared the hilltops to the east, its warm rays streamed through the windscreen. As the truck descended a steep hill, Charlie pumped the brakes. At the bottom was an inlet where small boats, some damaged and semi-submerged, were tied up. A short bridge spanned a channel that fed into a large inland sound. Over the bridge the road continued eastwards, now bordered to the north by the ocean and the turquoise waters of a shallow bay. In places there was vegetation, but many of the palms and casuarinas were distressed and dying as were the withered verges and expanses of brown that had once been grass. The plants had succumbed to the toxins and harsh bouts of radiation that periodically swept across the island.

After a series of hills and turnings, another stretch of water appeared. It was larger than the previous one they'd crossed. The shattered remains of a road causeway stretched away from the foreshore before fading to no little more than occasional stones poking through deeper water further out. The land on the far side was more than half-a-mile away.

Charlie turned the truck hard right down a narrow track. The lowest fronds of dying palms and palmettos brushed against the windshield and side windows. The undergrowth thickened as the track petered out. The truck stopped and Charlie turned off the engine.

Between the branches of the trees and the spindly limbs of mangroves there were glimpses of sparkling open water.

'Is this it?' Anna asked.

'This is where we switch.' Charlie jumped down, closing the driver's door behind him. By the time Anna joined him at the back of the truck he'd opened the door and was moving boxes of food and supplies to the rear edge. The only noise was the sliding of boxes along the floor and a few grunts from Charlie. Then Anna's ears pricked up.

'Something's out there,' she said.

Charlie stopped to listen. A twig snapped. He looked at Anna and raised a finger to his lips. Another twig snapped. He unclipped a metal bar from a corner of the truck and jumped down. The bar was rounded and almost as long as his arm. He wielded it like a club as he cautiously stepped forward. Anna followed, three steps behind. Branches in the underbrush suddenly shook violently. A figure came into view, stumbling to a crouch in the clearing. Charlie raised the metal bar, ready to strike, then dropped it to the ground and rushed forward.

'Lightfeather,' he said, gathering the collapsed woman into his arms.

'You know her?' Anna asked.

'She's one of us. She needs water.' Charlie flicked his head. 'There's some in the truck.'

The woman was carried to the side of the truck. Charlie placed her on the ground and took off his jacket to use as a pillow under her head. She moaned, her eyes were closed and her breathing shallow. Beads of sweat ran down Charlie's temples and cheeks. He faced Anna, but his eyes were focused in the mid-distance.

'Stay with her,' he said. He picked up the metal bar and used it to brush aside tree branches and plants as he strode into the underbrush.

'Where are you going?' Anna asked.

'Stay with her. Make sure she's okay. I'll be back in a few minutes. Shout if you hear or see anything.'

Anna watched him disappear into the tangle of palms, ferns and Mexican pepper bushes. She knelt beside Lightfeather and poured water from a plastic drink bottle onto a piece of cloth. She dabbed it against the woman's face, which had a light brown complexion. Lightfeather's eyes opened a fraction to reveal vibrant blue irises. She glanced upwards and moved her lips. At first there was no sound, then words tumbled out.

'It happened,' she mumbled.

'What happened?' asked Anna.

Lightfeather's eyes closed. She turned her head to one side, resting on the folded jacket. Strands of her fine, black hair lifted in the breeze then fell back onto the smooth skin of her cheek. Anna splashed more water onto the cloth and dabbed Lightfeather's face, lightly brushing the errant hair backwards. Then she stood up and looked around. A warm breeze threaded through the trees. She heard the heavier sound of branches being pushed aside and twigs snapping underfoot.

'Charlie?' she called. A moment later Charlie emerged from the bushes.

'The boat's there,' he said. 'How is she?'

'She's passing in and out.' Anna joined him at the rear of the truck. 'She needs medication. It's more than radiation sickness.'

Charlie threw the metal bar inside the truck. 'We'll get the supplies to the boat. The quicker we move, the better.'

He grabbed two boxes, stacking one on top of the other and carried them back the way he had come.

'She said something,' Anna blurted.

Charlie stopped. 'What did she say?'

'It happened. She said it happened.'

Charlie remained still for a moment, then plunged into the undergrowth. Between them they carried the boxes and supplies to a small boat tied up in a sandy bay bordered by a stand of mangroves. The boat had two onboard motors and enough room, when empty, for eight people. Once it was fully loaded, Lightfeather was carried aboard and laid down in the only space still free, beside the central console. Charlie untied the boat and powered up the motors. In moments they were speeding across the expanse of water towards a large stretch of land much further away than the crossing point at the destroyed causeway.

'Where are we?' Anna raised her voice to be heard above the drone of the motors.

'Castle Harbour,' Charlie replied as he steered, his eyes fixed on the horizon. 'It's two miles across. We keep the boat on the other side. Lightfeather ferried me across and knew to return after three days.'

'What did she mean when she said it happened?'

Charlie was silent. Anna brushed ocean spray from her face as the boat bounced across small waves, then repeated the question, louder.

'We'll see,' Charlie shouted back.

The rush of air against Anna's face was pleasant and cooling, countering the burning heat of the sun's unencumbered rays, but it faded as the boat slowed to approach a rocky shoreline.

'Cooper's Island,' Charlie announced, guiding the boat into an inlet near a crescent-shaped beach. 'It was used by the military and Nasa a long time ago.'

'A tracking station?'

'And other things.'

The boat was maneuvered into a shallow cove at the far end of the beach, where it was quickly hidden by wind-bent, steeply-angled branches of casuarinas. Lightfeather was carried from it and gently placed in a shaded sandy spot.

Charlie went to scale a nearby small incline. Anna stayed with Lightfeather and gazed up at the casuarinas as the wind whispered through their stunted and faded crisp brown needles. Parched wild grasses poking through the foreshore sand had lost their luster. She'd observed the distressed flora when she had first arrived, and on the journey from the city. It wasn't the semi-tropical climate that was responsible; it was the broiling climate and toxic storms.

She squatted and touched Lightfeather's face. Her skin was hot, too hot. She poured water from a drink bottle onto a cloth and dabbed it on her brow, then wiped some of the water on her own swollen eye, before putting the bottle down. Listening to the rhythmic rolling of the waves, she silently recalled memories of childhood vacations and became one with the surroundings as the quiet peacefulness wrapped itself around her. Then there was pain; a sharp crack against the back of her head. She fell forward, a weight forcing her into the sand. Straining to turn, she glimpsed an arm and a leg. Her face was forced into the ground. Sand fell into her mouth as she tried to shout. The hideous weight of her attacker pinned down her arms. She twisted her head and saw a dark shape and a flash of metal.

* * *

Opening her good eye, Anna saw blue sky through the thin branches of casuarinas. Her head throbbed, as did her arms. She was lying on her back and could feel cool sand against her hands. Cautiously she sat up, rubbing a swollen lump at the back of her head. Charlie and another man walked towards her. The stranger was heavy-set, bare-chested, with unkept brown hair reaching his shoulders. Charlie knelt beside her.

'How are you feeling?' he asked.

'I've been better. What happened?'

'Troy hit you.' Charlie's eyes gestured towards the other man standing a few paces away. 'He mistook you for an AI.'

Troy muttered an apology. Anna swiveled her right eye towards him.

'We have to get into the shelter. There are storm clouds approaching. We don't have much time,' said

Charlie. On cue, a crackle of thunder rippled through the air as the fringes of dark clouds peeked above the trees. Anna looked around. The boat had been pulled clear of the water and now rested on higher ground, camouflaged by a scattering of broken branches and palm fronds. The boxes of supplies were gone. There was an indentation in the sand where Lightfeather had lain.

'Where's Lightfeather?' she asked.

'In the shelter. We've taken everything there,' Charlie said, reaching down to help Anna to her feet. She managed without his assistance and stared at Troy, who responded with a nod of embarrassed acknowledgment. They walked for ten minutes through overgrown trails. Claps of thunder grew in volume and frequency as clouds snubbed out the sun and cast a twilight pall. Anna felt spits of rain on her head and hands and hoped it was not toxic or radioactive, but she knew it was probably both.

At first Anna didn't noticed the shelter. She, Charlie and Troy had emerged from a thicket of vegetation. Between two crooked casuarinas was a circular outline: it was the edge of a metal bunker, its outward facing wall flat and unadorned. A rusty iron door with peeling faded blue paintwork was the only indication that anything lay beyond. Troy pulled it open and ushered Anna and Charlie inside.

It took a moment for Anna's good eye and her partially swollen left eye to adjust to the dimly lit interior. A curved metal roof arched above, reaching a height of twenty feet. Suspended at regular intervals were a dozen florescent light tubes; three were illuminated. The cavernous shelter was sixty feet long and almost as wide. Stacked in small piles around the walls were the boxes that had been carried from the boat. Troy led the way to the far end of the shelter and another metal door. Rust scarred its hinges and edges. The word Nasa and the number 263 were stenciled on it. Anna wondered how long it had been since the old space agency had used the bunker.

Troy heaved the door open. 'Be prepared,' he said.

Anna followed Charlie into the next section of the bunker. As her sight adjusted to the darkness she saw the reason for Troy's warning.

CHAPTER FIVE

COOPER'S ISLAND

The storm left fingerprints. In shady areas among spindly casuarinas and young cedars, small puddles dotted the forest floor and droplets of rainwater dangled from leaves and branches. Anna walked slowly as she took in the surroundings and tried to make sense of what she'd seen. Although she was no longer vomiting, the bitter taste lingered. She gulped water from a bottle. The trail she was on snaked through the trees and palms.

At a high point the North Atlantic came into view, stretching away to the horizon and the dead world beyond. Anna sat down on an old concrete bench half hidden by drooping palm fronds. The swelling around her left eye had greatly reduced and she now had clear vision. The ocean claimed her attention. Her eyes defocused until the waves morphed and took on the appearance of a body rhythmically breathing. As a child she had imagined the Earth was alive and that the ocean's waves were its lungs. The metaphor stayed with her, but now the breathing of the waves was shallow and labored. In her contemplation - sitting alone sensing only the sun, the southerly breeze and the rise and fall of the waves - time had no meaning.

The spell was broken by the sound of footsteps through brittle grass. She turned and saw Charlie, his head bowed. He reached the bench and sat down beside her. She studied his face. She'd seen moments of sadness in his expression previously, but now there was also fear. She turned her attention back to the sea.

'Now we know what Lightfeather meant when she said it happened,' she said, placing her hands together, cradling her half-empty water bottle. 'I saw some mounds on the way here. Are those the others?'

'Yes,' said Charlie.

'And now five more to bury.' Anna ran a finger against her dry, cracking lips. 'The AIs don't need to find you. They know you're dying, like the rest of the island.'

Charlie stood up and stepped forward to look at the beach below.

'There's still life here. There's still hope,' he said

'Hope!' Anna was sardonic, but caught herself. 'The plants are dying. Look at their leaves, the color is draining from them. What's left of this greenery will be gone in weeks. There's no life out there, nothing. No insects, no birds.' The final word caught in her throat. She regained her composure, leant forward and pulled up a clump of grass. 'See how brittle it is. Everything's breaking down. Everything's poisoned, including us.'

'We have to try,' Charlie said. 'The four us.'

'Four?'

'I was counting you. Unless you don't plan on staying,' Charlie looked at her.

'As though there's a choice,' she breathed.

'Your friends, won't they come looking for you?'

'They're gone. I'll be presumed lost. The planetary quarantining is irreversible, it has to be. There won't be time for a search and rescue.'

'We'll still be here,' Charlie said.

'Not for long. The air we're breathing is probably killing us.' Anna took a pill from a pocket of her suit and swallowed it with a gulp of water.

'What's that?' Charlie asked.

'Iodine. I have a small supply.' She offered him a pill, he shook his head. 'Your shelter isn't enough,' she continued. 'Not for now, and not for what comes next.'

'And what's that?'

Anna stood and walked past him.

'The pulse,' she said.

'Pulse?'

'That's why no one's coming back for me.' She half-turned.

'Are you going to tell me more?' Charlie asked.

'There's no point.'

'Oh, there's a point.' Charlie vented. 'You think you're superior. Well, stop for one goddamn moment - for one lousy second - and think: what if you've got it wrong. What if there's a way to start again. What if it all goes wrong up there in your tin can space stations.'

At his feet there was a broken branch. He picked it up and snapped it in two.

'What if the answer is to start again right here, right now, to restore the Earth by working with it,' he continued.

'You're crazy.' Anna's words were measured and calm.

'Well maybe I am; me and the others.' Charlie hurled one half of the branch towards the distant ocean, followed by the other. 'You think there's only one solution: a sterile world with nothing for decades, centuries even, until you return along with whatever else manages to survive up there in space.'

'And what's your alternative?' Anna asked.

'Regenerating the world, re-seeding it without leaving. Assisting what's still here to re-establish a foothold. There have been mass extinctions before, but life finds a way.'

'Your idealism will be your downfall.' Anna looked him in the eye, then walked away.

'And your dogmatism will be yours,' Charlie shouted.

For the rest of the day Anna meandered through Cooper's Island, following old trails and exploring long-deserted buildings. She considered what Charlie had said, and her mind filled with clever counter arguments she could have used to bat back at him. When she was satisfied her internal logic had comprehensively squashed the views he presented, her restless mind sought further stimulus and annoyingly began to conjure up resolutions supporting Charlie's world vision. As she tried to shake them from her head she stumbled on a tree root, pivoting as she fell and throwing her hands forward to break the impact. For a moment she lay against the cool dirt, then pushed herself upwards. She noticed something on the ground; a bird's feather. Picking it up, she studied its intricate beauty and thought of the professor.

As evening approached the weather deteriorated. Dark, menacing rainclouds fanned out. Even without monitors or instrumentation Anna knew the rain would be acidic and radioactive; the only uncertainty was the degree of toxicity. The underground shelter afforded protection from the direct effects of a poisonous downpour, perhaps also from some of the radioactive dust. It might forestall the inevitable, she thought as she hurried along a barely visible path, ducking beneath limp branches and brown-edged palm fronds. She came to a clearing among the trees and stopped. Before her were the mounds of earth she'd seen earlier, but now expanded with five freshly disturbed plots. Had she arrived on the island a day or two earlier she might have met these souls who'd been so determined to avoid evacuation. Their dream of starting anew, of surviving and restoring the world, was now dust; as their bodies would soon be.

Lightning crackled against the bleak clouds. Large, warm drops of rain fell onto her head and hands as she ran. Emerging from the trees there was a speck of light illuminating the entrance to the shelter. She raced towards it in the thickening rain and crashed through the half-open door before falling to the ground. A dark figure held a small torch and reached down to pull her up. It was Charlie. He handed her a thick towel.

'Quick, dry yourself before the rain soaks in to your skin,' he urged.

Anna needed no instruction and vigorously dried herself, standing in the tiny pool of light provided by the torch. Flashes of lightning and booms of thunder filled the air outside. Charlie nudged the metal door shut.

'I'm sorry about earlier,' he said, turning to shine the torch towards the second doorway. As he and Anna neared the inner sanctum he stopped. 'There's some more bad news,' he warned.

In the second chamber four spotlights positioned in the corners directed light at a central spot where Troy rested on a chair in a circle of eight. The other seven chairs were empty. To his right a white sheet shrouded the body of Lightfeather. Anna shuddered. She and Charlie joined Troy and sat in silence for a long moment.

Charlie finally spoke. 'If we hadn't been forced from the other place, we would have been safe.'

Troy nodded. Anna studied their faces, they had their heads half bowed, looking at the dusty floor.

'What place?' she asked.

'Another shelter, like this, but new,' Charlie said. 'This one's a hundred years old, or more. It was built in the Twentieth century, then it was abandoned.'

Troy took up the narrative. 'Before the wars began a new shelter was built, equipped with air filtration systems, mini nuclear power units - the works.'

'That's where we stayed when we ran,' Charlie interjected. 'It was a haven. No one fell sick. But the AIs raided the shelter and took the nuclear material. We were forced to hide again.'

Anna ran her fingers through her damp hair. 'Is everything gone?'

'Pretty much. Troy and his group made sorties to see what was happening. The shelter is bare and damaged. The AIs made sure it could never be used again.'

'Then it's just a matter of time.' Anna dropped her hands onto her lap. 'This place can protect from the acid rain, but the air coming in is contaminated.'

Charlie walked to the edge of the chamber and opened a box of supplies. He grabbed a packet of cookies and ripped open the wrapper as he returned. He offered the treats. Troy took a handful, Anna declined. A crash of thunder reverberated through the shelter.

'How long has it been since you left the other place?' Anna asked.

'Four weeks, maybe five,' said Charlie as he sat down. 'I hadn't expected us to lose so many good people so quickly. Sometimes, I wish we hadn't run.'

There was silence. One of the corner lights flickered and went out, birthing new shadows to shade their solemn faces.

'Why are the AIs here. What made them choose Bermuda as a base?' Charlie asked.

'They've been eradicated in most other places, or should have been,' said Anna. 'Bermuda's remote enough to have escaped the electromagnetic bombardments.'

'Electromagnetic bombardment - wouldn't that destroy infrastructure?' asked Troy.

'Yes,' Anna replied. 'Electronics and anything that relies on electricity. It's a scorched earth solution. That's why the evacuation was necessary for anyone hoping to survive long enough to see the atmosphere stabilize and regenerate. If it ever does.'

'And the AIs don't want anyone to escape,' Charlie summed up.

'They view us as the cause of the world's destruction, the reason it is in tatters,' said Anna. 'The logic follows that if they eradicate mankind then the first part of a solution is achieved.'

Charlie grunted. 'Well, Troy has something to tell you.'

Troy finished eating a cookie and cleared his throat. 'There might be a way out. There's two old aircraft and a jet craft at the airport. The jet was left behind when the evacuation shuttle departed.'

'What kind of jet?' Anna asked.

'I'm not sure. When I was out that way a few days ago I saw the AIs doing something to it. Maybe it's something you can fly.'

* * *

Anna had a fitful sleep. She awoke several times and in the darkness listened to the silence. The storm had passed. Her mind was unsettled, filled with the possibilities presented by the jet craft at the airport. Was it a scramjet? Was it capable of orbital ascent? She had previously resigned herself to her fate on the dying world. Now she sensed a possible escape.

In the morning she helped carry the body of Lightfeather to the burial patch. Troy and Charlie dug a shallow grave. There was a simple ceremony with words from Troy, who had known Lightfeather since childhood. Anna's thoughts drifted to her own days of youth and the carefree explorations she and her best friend found to fill summers; summers that seemed to stretch for ever. As the memories danced, she gazed at the sky through the branches of the casuarinas and for a fleeting moment thought she saw a bird. But when she concentrated there was nothing there. An illusion, she told herself, her mind projecting something that was missing, trying to make the world whole again.

There had been very little conversation during the morning's sombre task. When they returned to the shelter the activity level stepped up. They agreed to go to the airport and see the jet craft.

After setting out and walking for half an hour they reached an area of rough grass. Troy and Charlie scrambled across it and picked their way over jagged rocks on the shoreline, then beckoned Anna to follow. As she did, her wrist monitor vibrated. It was a countdown alert indicating thirty-six hours until the imposition of planetary quarantine. She refocused. The foreshore was a formidable maze of razor-sharp rock formations that had been eroded by centuries of wind, rain and waves. She threaded her way through the stones, boulders and a number of long-redundant cylindrical concrete structures. There was a small climb up an embankment of scree to reach a chainlink fence that marked the airfield perimeter.

Crouching, Anna, Charlie and Troy scanned the barren airfield. The terminal building, its glass facade sparkling in the sun, was a mile away. There was no sign of activity. Two commercial aircraft were parked in front of the terminal. Access hatches on the planes' fuselages and wings hung open. Troy nudged Anna and pointed at something to the right of the planes. Through a pair of binoculars she recognized its shape.

'A scramjet!' She could barely believe it. In single file they skirted the perimeter fence until they found a spot where the chainlink had been damaged and untidily pulled to the side to create a small gap. Anna crawled through. Charlie followed, but Troy hesitated. He slipped onto an elbow, his breathing labored.

'You okay?' Charlie asked.

A film of sweat glistened across Troy's brow and trickled from his temples.

'I just need a minute,' he answered. His eyes were glazed and he avoided looking at the others. Pulling away from the fence, he twisted his body as he tried to stand. He managed two unsteady steps then bent over and vomited, before slumping into a seated position with his back to the fence.

'It's the sickness,' Anna said to Charlie. 'He needs to go back. I'll go on alone.'

Charlie crawled through the fence and helped Troy to his feet. He faced Anna. 'You sure about this?' he asked.

Anna nodded and turned, jogging away towards the terminal and the planes. Reaching the first of the commercial airliners, she crouched and looked back along the airfield. She could no longer see Charlie or Troy. She turned her attention to the terminal, searching for activity. There was none. The only sound was a metallic scraping as the access hatch doors on the planes swung gently in the breeze.

Anna scurried across the tarmac and ducked down beside the wheels of the nearest plane to check all was clear before moving to the second aircraft. Now the scramjet was in full view. She darted from the cover of the plane to the side of the scramjet and twisted a clamp on a manual mechanism panel on the craft's undercarriage. The panel slid open, revealing four buttons. The activation sequence for the main door was a fleet generic code that she automatically recalled. Her reward was a hydraulic hiss as the main hatch opened.

The inside of the scramjet was identical to her own, but its AI control system had been uninstalled - the first item she checked. Without it, the craft could only be flown manually and there was no way to transmit or receive communications.

It took her a full hour to thoroughly check the scramjet's systems and equipment. When she was done, she reclined in the pilot seat and contemplated an identity card wedged into a gap on the dashboard. It belonged to Captain Ricardo Menzies. She did not know him, but had found his flight schedule. He had been tasked with assisting the exodus mission. There was no sign of him in the scramjet. His exoskeleton suit still hung in its storage rack. Wherever he was, he had left the protective kit behind; an unwise move, if it had been a choice, thought Anna. She was thankful to have found it. She'd tried it on for size and now intended to wear it for all outdoor activity. The island's atmosphere was toxic and unstable, and the rapid deterioration of Lightfeather had been shocking. A cocktail of airborne radiation and poisons were impacting with brutality. She dreaded to think about what she had been exposed to since arriving. Through the cockpit window she stared at the airfield. Two droids appeared on the tarmac below. They were AIs -

Sym-54s - and they loaded two large missiles into the cargo hold of one of the airliners.

A dusky sunset bathed the island by the time Anna returned to the shelter. She was encased in Captain Ricardo's exoskeleton suit, and had forged a few shortcuts on her return to the bunker, utilizing the suit's powerful arm hydraulics to scythe through dense vegetation and fallen tree trunks.

At the outer entrance to the shelter Charlie raised his pistol at the appearance of the suited figure. He lowered it when he heard Anna's voice and saw her face through the glass visor of the helmet.

Anna removed the helmet inside the first chamber of the shelter and stepped out of the exoskeleton suit at the entrance to the second, leaving it standing rigid beside the door where it gave the appearance of a fourth person in the shelter. Bright light from the reenergized corner spot lamps bathed two chairs in the middle of the chamber, which were next to the camp bed where Lightfeather had rested the day before. It was now occupied by Troy. Anna joined Charlie at the chairs.

'How did it go?' Charlie asked.

'Interesting. And worrying.' Anna stood and faced him, resting her hands on the back of a chair. 'But first, how's Troy?'

'He's been sleeping for a few hours. He threw up continuously on the way back, and drank a lot of water before he fell asleep - just like Lightfeather.'

Anna knelt beside Troy and brushed the back of her right hand against his forehead, feeling the heat within.

'High fever. Prepare for the worst.'

Charlie nodded. 'It's happening so quickly. It was a drawn out deterioration before. What's changed?'

Anna sat on a chair and sipped water from a bottle. 'There's been an increase in radiation and whatever other lethal toxins are in those storms,' she said. 'Without telemetry it's hard to know how bad it's become.'

A loud bang shook the ground and walls of the shelter.

'Thunder?' Charlie said.

'Let's hope so.'

'So, the airport. What did you discover?'

Anna gathered her thoughts. 'The scramjet's in good shape.'

'You'll be able to fly it?'

'Partly,' Anna replied. 'The onboard AI control system has been removed. I can fly it manually, but without communication and without a fully functioning computer there's no way I'd be able to locate the escape corridor.'

'What's that?'

'A safe passage from the Earth. Anything outside its precise coordinates is destroyed; it has to be that way. The rogues wouldn't hesitate to launch an assault on the stations if they could get beyond the orbital defenses.'

'Then there's no way out for you either?'

'Maybe. If I fly that scramjet to where mine crashed, I can transfer what's missing.'

'And you can escape.'

'*WE* can,' Anna corrected him. 'It'll be a squeeze, but we'll get the three of us onboard. We don't have much time.' She looked at her watch. 'Less than twenty hours.'

'What happens after that? You said something before - the pulse - but you never explained.'

Anna sighed and scanned the dimly lit chamber.

'You can't tell me?' Charlie stared at her, seeking a clue from her expression. 'What, you think we're bugged?'

'It's critical the rogue AIs don't know.' Anna locked her eyes on Charlie's. 'Outside of Artemis Control I'm the only one with the information, and that's as far as the risk goes.'

'If it's going to affect my survival I should know,' Charlie huffed.

'It's not. You're going to be with me.'

There was a long silence, the only sound was water dripping somewhere in the first chamber.

Eventually Charlie spoke. 'Did you see any droids?'

Anna frowned. 'Two. They were loading one of the planes with some old-style missiles. They put them in the cargo hold.'

'Missiles. How?'

'They must have been brought to the island. Who knows where from. When they left, I checked the destination of the plane's automated flight plan: it's New York, tomorrow. The controls were locked down.'

'Why there? That place was destroyed years ago,' Charlie asked.

Anna stared at the dusty ground around the camp bed where Troy slept, but said nothing.

'If they're going to destroy something that's already been destroyed, then I guess we just leave them to it,' Charlie added.

Movement flickered in Anna's peripheral vision. She looked up into the darkness. Something lightly brushed against her hairline. She checked with her hand, but there was nothing.

'We have to disable it,' she said, refocusing on Charlie.

'You know something. Something about New York. What is it? Another thing you can't tell me?'

Anna sighed.

'I thought we were the only ones,' Charlie persisted. 'Are there others in New York?'

Thunder reverberated through the shelter. They listened to its diminishing echo.

'There are others, right?' Charlie repeated.

There was no reply.

Charlie huffed. 'Something else you aren't able to speak about? Okay, tell me this: the scramjet, does it have weapons?'

Anna shook her head. 'No. The terrestrial mission scramjets are unarmed for safety, in case they fall into the wrong hands.'

Charlie thought for a moment. 'Then we'll have to destroy the plane with explosives,' he said.

'Where from?'

'The quarry. It's basic stuff, dynamite, but there's enough if we can get it to the airport.'

'We need to start early,' said Anna. 'The plane's automated takeoff is noon.'

'We'll take the boat to the main island an hour before dawn. I can navigate in the …'

'No,' Anna interrupted. 'We'll take scramjet. I have a plan.'

CHAPTER SIX

THE PLAN

It wasn't part of the plan to be woken during the night by Troy's cries of pain. Anna and Charlie tended to him, carefully pouring cold water from bottles against his overheating skin, and coaxing him to drink. He was unable to keep any of it down. His eyes were dilated. Anna and Charlie reassured him that he was not alone. He drifted back to sleep, but the scene was repeated twice more.

Then it was over.

At three in the morning - the agreed start of the day for what lay ahead - Anna checked on Troy. She couldn't find his pulse.

'He's gone,' she said. For several minutes she and Charlie sat in silence. Then Charlie pulled the sheet over Troy's head.

'We'd better go if we're to have enough time,' he said.

After eating a simple breakfast they left. At the doorway of the inner chamber, Anna climbed into the exoskeleton suit and lowered the helmet's visor before turning and looking back. The corner spotlights cast a shadowy light on the two chairs and Troy's shrouded body. She took in the scene, knowing she might not return. Outside the shelter, she and Charlie paused to take in their surroundings. The night sky was alive with the pinpricks of a thousand stars.

'Okay, let's do this,' said Charlie. He lead the way, except for sections where Anna showed shortcuts she had forged the previous evening. Night's inky black was fading to a deep blue when they reached the airfield perimeter. The eastern horizon was tinged a predawn red as they crouched by the gap in the fence.

'Looks all clear,' Anna said.

Charlie continued his sweep of the airfield with binoculars, then crawled through the gap to join Anna. Each minute brought an incremental brightening of the surroundings as the stenciled red line of dawn expanded and changed hue, firstly to orange then yellow. They jogged towards the terminal where the planes and scramjet were parked on the airfield apron. Anna felt clumsy in the exoskeleton suit. For all its superior strength it barely allowed a pace faster than a walk. She took the lead as they approached the planes, darting to the wheels below the undercarriage of the nearest. She knelt and checked for activity. With Charlie in tow she flitted to the next plane, and finally to the scramjet.

Once inside and free from the confines of the exoskeleton suit, Anna showed Charlie where best to position himself in the craft that was designed to hold only one occupant. He braced his arms and legs against the walls in the rear cabin, while Anna sat in the pilot seat and activated the controls.

'You all set?' she called.

'Let's do it,' Charlie replied. He could see into the cockpit and, over the shoulder of Anna, the dim outline of the runway outside. The scramjet's engines fired up and the craft lifted vertically into the air. Charlie fought to maintain his braced position against the rapid momentum. The first rays of daylight shafted through the cockpit as the airborne craft turned and headed towards the main island. As it flew over the terminal building Anna imagined the AIs below wondering how the cannibalised scramjet, shorn of its computerized control systems, had taken flight. She kept the altitude at 150 feet above Castle Harbour as Charlie shouted out directions to the quarry, which was near the waterside on the opposite side from Cooper's Island.

'There it is. Down there,' Charlie said. Anna tilted the scramjet to get a better view of a scarred hillside nestled between trees and palms. She landed the scramjet vertically in a clearing beside three small buildings on the edge of the earthworks.

Charlie was eager to disembark. As soon as the hatch door opened and the ramp lowered he dashed out, but he stopped a short distance from the scramjet, doubled over and vomited. By the time Anna had put on the exoskeleton suit and followed him, Charlie had straightened up. His eyes were watering and he had a pained expression. 'I'm okay,' he weakly reassured.

'You're not.' Anna handed him an iodine tablet. 'You should stay in the ship. I'll fetch the explosives. Tell me where they are.'

'No, I'll be fine. It'll be quicker if I show you.' Charlie marched towards a blue hut a short distance away from the other buildings. Its metal blast door was similar to those at the shelter. He tried to pull it open, but it didn't budge. Anna grabbed the handle and using the enhanced strength of her suit levered the lock until it buckled and snapped. The door swung aside and Charlie jumped into the dark interior. Moments later he emerged carrying a metal box.

'There's three more. Can you carry these?'

'Bring them all, we'll take them in one journey,' said Anna, taking the box from him.

Charlie could manage only one at a time, but Anna stacked all four and using the suit's power-assist lifted and carried them to the scramjet. Charlie followed, sweating and breathless and stumbling across the dusty yard. Back inside the scramjet, Anna handed him a bottle of water, which he drank empty.

'I know, I know. It's happening.' He wiped his lips. 'I can last long enough to get this done.'

'You need to wear an exosuit. There's another one at my ship,' said Anna.

'Have you got an iodine pill?'

Anna dipped a hand in her pocket and pulled out the last pill, along with a bird feather. It was the feather she'd collected from the ground when she had fallen the previous day. She handed Charlie the pill.

Sitting on the boxes of explosives, Charlie resumed his brace position in the heart of the scramjet as it took off and darted westwards. Anna intended to use the distant tall buildings and glass dome of Hamilton as a way-mark to trace the route back to her beached scramjet. But she was distracted by the small feather, which she had wedged upright into a thin crack at the top of the control dashboard.

'Why are we landing?' asked Charlie.

The scramjet descended vertically at the edge of the city dome.

'There's something I need,' Anna said.

Suddenly, a towering figure, arms raised, filled the cockpit window. Anna gasped and jerked back in her seat.

'Jeepers!'

'Johnny Barnes,' declared Charlie.

'Who?' Anna regained her composure, realizing the figure outside was a larger than life-size bronze statue of a bearded man wearing a wide-brimmed hat and frozen in a double-handed wave. Smiling.

'Johnny Barnes,' Charlie repeated. 'A man before my time.'

'A great one?' Anna unbuckled from the seat.

'Not in the way others gained statues. A regular guy. For the last thirty years of his life he stood at the side of the road waving at commuters and sending them love. I was told about him as a kid.'

'Was he paid to do it?'

'No. He did it because he wanted to. Mr Happy Man. Gee, what I'd give to feel that unconditional love now.'

Anna studied the features of the statue outside the window, then turned and squeezed past Charlie. She put on the exoskeleton suit and opened the hatch.

'You stay in the ship. I'll be quick,' she said.

Charlie switched places and sat in the pilot seat. Through the window he watched Anna march past the bronze statue and enter an opening in the dome, vanishing into the city beyond.

It was fifteen minutes before she returned, carrying the limp, humanoid body of the Sym-54 droid that Charlie had shot the evening they met. She bundled the inactive AI into a corner of the scramjet.

'Okay, it's going to be a tighter squeeze,' she said.

'What do you want that for?' asked Charlie, as he unsteadily relinquished the pilot seat.

'It has a use.'

'Well, having it in here makes me nervous.' Charlie stared at the broken droid as he resumed his position seated on the boxes of explosives.

'Don't worry,' Anna reassured. 'You finished it off real good.'

The scramjet lifted into the morning sky. As it climbed the full sweep of the glass dome sprawled before it. Anna squinted to shield her eyes from the glare and turned the scramjet towards the island's southern coastline. She stayed alert for danger, aware that it had been surprisingly easy to take the scramjet from the airport. Were the AIs so confident that they considered a few stragglers, a few dying 'runners', of minimal concern, she wondered. The flight to the beach took less than a minute.

The sea sparkled and high on the golden sands was the damaged scramjet. Circling above, Anna checked all was clear in the vicinity, then landed next to the crashed craft. As the hum of the engines died away she turned and saw Charlie spluttering and coughing, unable to vomit but clearly in pain.

'We need you inside a suit,' she said.

Anna donned the exoskeleton suit and exited the scramjet. Charlie followed, stopping twice to bend over, hands on thighs, as he gathered his strength.

Standing outside her wrecked scramjet, Anna spoke into the helmet's microphone.

'Sheean, can you hear me?'

'Yes, commander,' replied the AI.

'I'm outside. Open the door.'

Hydraulics hissed and the hatch opened. As soon as she was inside, she took off the exoskeleton suit and pointed to it as Charlie staggered aboard.

'This is yours now,' she said. 'Wear it at all times when you're outside.'

With some difficulty Charlie stepped into the suit. Anna's personal exoskeleton suit was still hanging in the crashed scramjet. She unhooked it and put it on.

'Okay, can you hear me?' she asked through the helmet microphone.

'Yes,' replied Charlie.

'Good. Start preparing the explosives. I'm going to transfer the AI system from this ship and install it in the other.'

Charlie took his first awkward steps in the bulky suit, exiting down the ramp and onto the beach.

'Wow, this is like power walking,' he declared.

'Be careful,' Anna called, then addressed the onboard AI. 'Sheean, the AI hub on the other ship has been removed. I need to migrate you. Can you connect wirelessly?'

'LiFi transfer is possible if auxiliary ports are aligned,' Sheean responded.

'I'll do it.'

Two small external portals on each scramjet were opened and an optic prism was targeted from one to the other. Once the prisms were synced, the transfer of data through a full spectrum laser commenced. The entire process took twelve minutes. Anna was in the pilot seat of Captain Ricardo's scramjet when Sheean informed her the migration was complete. She turned to Charlie, who was in the rear cabin sorting through the boxes of explosives.

'We're good to go. You ready?' she asked.

'Almost.' He closed the lid on the top box.

'Will it work?'

'The material's old, but it's in fair condition. If it's inside the plane it'll blow the fuselage wide open.'

'All we need is to get inside,' Anna said. 'It won't be easy. Those droids will be active now.'

As the scramjet rose from the beach to begin the return journey, Anna instructed Sheean to attempt communication with Artemis Control. However, the impenetrable atmospheric storms made that impossible. Sheean suggested that a signal to a low orbiting relay satellite might be picked up.

Anna began recording. 'Artemis Control, this is a relayed message from Gold Commander. Planetary quarantine is T-minus four hours and thirty-three minutes. I'm in Bermuda. My scramjet was disabled. I've commandeered another; it belonged to Captain Ricardo. I do not know where he is, or what has happened to him.'

She paused and stared out of the cockpit at the rooftops of homes below, they appeared as white dots scattered amongst the dying greenery. The scramjet was at treetop-height hugging the southern coastline.

'I made contact with runners on the island. Only one has survived the deteriorating conditions,' Anna continued the message. 'Intend to exit planet before quarantine. Please stand by. Over.'

The scramjet reached the eastern-most outcrop of Bermuda. Anna recognized Cooper's Island, with the small trails she had walked, and the casuarina-covered hillock that housed the shelter. She dipped the craft low above gently rolling waves near the shoreline and picked a landing spot on a short sliver of beach near to the airfield and out of sight of the airport terminal.

She and Charlie rebooted into their exoskeleton suits. The hatch door opened and they exited down the ramp.

'Sheean, end all communications and signaling telemetry until I return. Lock hatch and open only on my command,' Anna said.

She turned to Charlie. Sweat was beading around his temples, and his breathing was strained as he carried the boxes of explosives.

'You okay?' she asked.

'Let's do this,' he affirmed.

'We'll keep our person-to-person channel open on short range. If we're within one hundred feet of each other we'll be able to communicate. Anything greater will be intercepted by the AIs.'

They shared the boxes and followed a scratchy trail through brittle wild grass along the outer edge of the airfield. Once through the gap in the fence they made their way stealthily towards the terminal, stopping and crouching at intervals to observe their surroundings. They spotted only a single droid. It moved beside one of the commercial jets, checking the fuselage and exterior doors before vanishing around a far corner of the terminal.

Anna and Charlie scurried beneath the first plane, then to the second where they rested against its wheel arches. At the rear was a cargo hatch, which Anna opened. She pulled herself inside. Charlie passed up the boxes of explosives before joining her.

A piercing spotlight on the righthand side of Anna's helmet provided enough illumination to reveal the dark outlines of two rusted, ten-foot long missiles resting in the cargo hold. Charlie knelt beside one and rubbed a gloved hand against its corroded casing to reveal Cyrillic lettering.

'Russian!' he gasped.

'Soviet.' Anna pointed at a faded, painted image of a flag. 'That makes them more than a century old.'

They inspected the missiles.

'Why would there be Soviet missiles here?' Anna asked.

'There was something I was taught in history class,' said Charlie. 'A nuclear submarine sank a few hundred miles from Bermuda, a long time ago. It ended up on the seabed two or three miles down, too deep to be retrieved.'

'Not for the AIs.' Anna checked a device on the cuff of her suit. 'Plutonium-239 isotopes. Keep your suit on. This stuff is forever radioactive.'

'Forever?'

'It'll take tens of thousands of years to decay.'

Charlie coughed. 'How long do we have?'

'Twenty minutes until take-off.'

Charlie began unpacking the first explosives.

'I'm going to confirm the flight program hasn't altered,' said Anna. 'Can you manage alone?'

Charlie had one hand full of tubes of explosives, he gave a thumbs up with the other.

A door at the front of the cargo hold opened to a small set of internal steps, which Anna climbed to reach a pressurized door. On the other side she found herself in the passenger cabin with rows of empty seats either side of a central aisle. She squeezed along it, her exoskeleton suit brushing against the tightly packed seats. Rays of sunshine fanned through porthole windows that afforded glimpses of the featureless airport tarmac. The cockpit cabin door was slightly ajar, exactly as she had left it during her sortie the previous day. She entered the flight-deck, her eyes darting from left to right. Nothing had changed. She pressed a button to activate the central screen console. It displayed the flight schedule. The departure time was still noon and the destination was unchanged: Manhattan.

She sat down on one of the pilot seats and stared out of the window at the runway. The airfield was shimmering in the heat. In a few hours this would all be a memory, and she'd be at Artemis Control or one of the lunar stations, debriefing. Charlie would be assimilating back into the society he'd once forsaken. And this - this remote island - would be left to its fate along with the rest of the planet, engulfed in swirling, toxic storms. The Earth would be put to sleep, for now and perhaps forever. She cursed as she stared at the world outside and strained for a fragment of hope - an animal scurrying across the airfield, a bird darting across the breathless sky, even an inquisitive insect crawling on the window. But there was none. She defocused, allowing her imagination to show her what was missing, what she craved.

'Damn us,' she whispered, wiping at nebulous tears.

When she returned to the cargo hold, Charlie was frantically wiring up the explosives against the inner fuselage. He looked up as she approached.

'There's a problem.' He was blunt. 'Everything's primed, but the triggering device is kaput.'

'How?'

'Who knows how long it's been lying in that old storeroom. The explosives will need to be manually triggered.' He stood to face her. 'Someone's going to have to stay onboard.'

'That would be suicide,' said Anna.

They stared at each other through their visors. Charlie was sweating. His eyes were bloodshot and feverishly weeping at the edges. He coughed.

'It's the only way to stop this payload,' he said. 'Unless we disable the plane on the ground. We've got these suits, we could do some damage ...'

'No. If anything happens to this plane or its flight systems the AIs would be here in an instant. We might stop it flying, but we'd be finished,' Anna said.

'Even in these suits?'

'The AIs know the weaknesses. We wouldn't survive long.'

'Long enough for me to pop a few.' Charlie took his pistol from a hip pocket.

'And how many bullets do you have. Two?' Anna asked. 'There'll be more than two of them.'

Charlie sighed, his legs wobbled and he sat down. 'So what's it to be. We save ourselves or we save whatever's in New York that's so important you can't tell me?'

Anna was silent.

'How long do we have? Ten minutes?' Charlie's breathing was rapid and shallow. 'It's okay, you can tell me what's there, I'm not going to snitch to the AIs in ten minutes.'

'That's not why. If they caught you, they'd extract the information regardless.' Anna knelt next to him. 'You're deteriorating fast. We need to get you....

Charlie waved her away. 'Those AIs wouldn't be going to this trouble if they didn't already know. There's people, right?'

Anna flicked her gaze around the cargo hold to double-check they were alone, but said nothing.

'If I'm going to die I'd like to know what for,' said Charlie as he resumed wiring the explosives.

'Who said you're going to die?' Anna was abrupt.

Charlie coughed and dry retched. His eyes were reddened and glazed, beads of sweat dripped from his forehead. He gestured towards the explosives.

'I'm staying onboard to detonate them.'

'I'm not leaving you to do that,' Anna said.

'You are, and you will. I belong here. It's too late for me. You go, do what you have to do. How long now?'

Anna checked her watch. 'Five minutes.'

'Go. Don't make this all for nothing.'

Even in her helmet Anna could smell the dust of the aircraft's interior, the salty rust that clung to the ancient missiles, and the sickening perfuse sweat that signaled Charlie's terminal condition. She turned and left, looking back only when she had reached the rear cargo bay hatch. Charlie was slumped on the floor, gripping the firing mechanism for the explosives, his visor steamed up by his feverous heat.

'There's a man,' Anna said.

'A man! All this for one man.' Charlie laughed. It was a weak laugh.

'And birds.'

'Birds!' Charlie coughed violently, rattling his body. He called out as Anna closed and locked the hatch. His words were faint, but she heard them.

The tarmac apron was deserted as she dashed into the shadows of the terminal building. She watched as the airplane, under automated control, taxied towards the runway. Charlie's final words replayed in her mind as she crept beside the perimeter fence towards the gap, stopping once to watch the airplane takeoff.

'Good luck, and thank you,' she said softly.

By the time she reached the scramjet the plane had vanished into dark clouds to the northwest. She fired up the scramjet's engines and once airborne skimmed the craft above the airfield as it gained altitude. From the corner of her eye she saw two droids scurry from the terminal. Seconds later a projectile screeched past the cockpit then twisted back on itself.

'Sheean, what is it?'

'Homing missile. Locked on.'

'Can we evade?'

'Assuming full control. Brace for G-force,' said Sheean.

Anna gritted her teeth. The scramjet performed a sharp left turn, then it shot directly upwards before plummeting nose-first towards the runway. Anna tried to scream, but pinned by immense G-forces could not. Her world suddenly turned black. She did not see the scramjet pull out of its plumb trajectory with inches to spare, nor did she see the pursuing missile fail to replicate the extreme aerodynamic maneuver and, with explosive finality, smash into the ground. She did not see any of it. Her body was ragged, her consciousness stolen by spine-snapping G-forces.

CHAPTER SEVEN

THE RETURN

When Anna regained consciousness her vision was blurred, but she could tell that the scramjet was flying above clouds that swirled menacingly. Sitting up from a slumped position, she reorientated.

'Sheean, status report.'

'Present location above North Atlantic, near coast of South Carolina,' the onboard AI replied.

'And the missile?'

'Homing missile impacted on runway at Bermuda airport.'

'How long was I out?'

'You were unconscious for eighteen minutes.'

Anna gathered her thoughts and rubbed her eyes. There was a blinding flash to the righthand side of the scramjet. She turned, searching for its source. A plume of cloud and flame spread rapidly across the northern horizon.

'Increasing altitude. Brace for incoming shockwaves,' Sheean warned. The scramjet shot upwards, the sky turned an inky blue and the curvature of the Earth became evident. The craft rocked violently.

'The plane?' Anna asked.

'Affirmative. Airborne nuclear detonation one hundred miles north of Bermuda, altitude four miles.'

A second shockwave pushed against the scramjet.

'Where are we heading?'

'Coordinates for evacuation corridor. Arrival in ten minutes.'

Anna twisted her wrist to view the monitor watch. Planetary quarantine was less than an hour away.

'Sheean, disengage autopilot.' She took control and turned the scramjet northwards. There was a buzz on the communications panel.

'Incoming signal from Artemis Control,' Sheean notified.

'Don't acknowledge. Maintain silence.'

'Procedural irregularity. Resuming auto-control.'

'No!' Anna shouted. She gripped the joystick, but was unable to manipulate it; the AI had control.

'Sheean, I need you with me.' Anna lowered her voice. 'There's something left to do.'

'Your behavior indicates concussion.'

'I'm fine. We'll contact Artemis Control shortly.'

Sheean was silent. A thin red laser beam was projected from the control panel onto Anna's face. She blinked, then widened her eyes as the beam scanned her pupils. The laser switched off.

'Well?'

After a long wait, Anna felt responsiveness return to the control joystick.

'Manual control restored,' Sheean confirmed.

'Thank you,' Anna breathed. The scramjet raced towards the blanket of clouds that obliterated the view below, then plunged into the swirling maelstrom.

Crackling bolts of lightning flashed in all directions as the scramjet descended into a twilight world. Clouds hung low above the ground. Ahead was the outline of Manhattan's shattered dome and within it the remains of skyscrapers jutting upwards. The scramjet banked as Anna honed in on Eighth Avenue in the heart of the destroyed city.

Once landed, it took only ten minutes to find the metro station building and the hole in the wall that led to its deserted entrance plaza. The air tasted acrid inside the concealed subway. Anna slowly descended the four flights of stairs to the underground platform. She had left her exoskeleton suit outside the building in order to squeeze through the hole in the wall. No longer benefiting from its power, she now struggled to drag the body of the destroyed Sym-54 droid that she had recovered in Hamilton. At the bottom of the final set of stairs she cautiously stepped onto the station platform. In the dim emergency lighting, the outline of Humbro emerged. The AI droid was propped up against a wall, in almost the same place where it had been when she'd fired her flare pistol at it days before.

'Who are you?' it called out.

'Commander Anna.' She gently dropped the limp Sym-54 she was dragging onto the ground. Humbro's robotic eyes glowed red in the shadows, observing her approach.

'You've come for Professor Dale, and the birds,' it said. Anna knelt beside the droid.

'Where is the professor?' she asked.

'He's dead.'

'How?'

'He crawled back inside from where you left him. He went to his workshop and never returned.'

Humbro's orb eyes stared into Anna's. She felt ill, consumed by tortured thoughts.

'Maybe he's alright,' she said. 'Where's his workshop?'

'No.' Humbro's voice was flat. 'He's gone. The birds know.'

A sparrow landed on the concrete floor a few feet away, silently observing Anna and Humbro.

'The birds told you?'

The AI ignored the question and asked its own. 'Why didn't you take him?'

'Something happened; I had to leave.' Anna's gaze dropped to the ground.

'And now you're here for the birds. That's your mission: rescue them, take them to die on a space station.'

'No,' Anna replied quietly.

'No? What kind of commander would you be if you left them. How would you explain that?'

Anna lifted her head and peered into Humbro's glowing eyes. 'Time has run out. The evacuation corridor is about to be terminated.' She paused. 'I'm the last. We will not return.'

'Then they have a chance.'

'How? Without the professor, without you, they'll die just like everything that's out there.'

Humbro's eyes dimmed. The sparrow chirped.

'You have something,' the AI said.

'A broken Sym-54.' Anna looked across at the expired droid resting further along the platform. 'I hoped Professor Dale could salvage parts to fix you.'

For more than a minute neither spoke, then Humbro broke the silence.

'You can do the repair.'

'I'm a pilot, not a technician.'

'I'll instruct. You'll need the professor's tools from his workshop at the end of the platform.'

Anna stood and walked towards the far end of the platform. There was an open door. She entered a room that was lit by a single ceiling bulb. Slumped on a chair was the professor. With trepidation she approached and rested a hand on his chest. His skin was ghastly pale, his lifeless eyes open. She felt nauseous and backed away, snatching up the toolkit that rested on a nearby workbench.

She returned to the platform and removed the burnt and shattered panel on Humbro, replacing it with one from the Bermuda droid. Humbro gave her detailed instructions.

As she worked, Anna spoke about the fate of the runners in Bermuda.

'The last one, Charlie - his final words to me were to save the birds,' she said.

Humbro remained focused on guiding the repair, telling Anna to cross two red wires and pair them with an orange connector. She did so.

'Will they survive?' she asked.

'The birds?' said Humbro. 'Either they will, or they won't. If I'm able to help them, that improves their chances.'

Anna twisted her arm to check her watch.

'Your time is short,' Humbro observed.

'Yes., I'll need to ….'

'Go. You should, and now.' Humbro suddenly moved both arms and shifted its legs. Anna jumped to her feet in shock.

'It worked!' she said.

Humbro rose to its feet. 'I'll be able to finish things. It's time for you to leave.'

Anna faced the AI. 'There's something I need to know. The professor spoke about the birds surviving after the dinosaurs died.'

'That's why they have a chance to survive again.' Humbro held out a metallic arm. A robin flew out from the platform's shadows and settled on one of the AI's extended finger digits. 'They're agile. They can travel great distances to find pockets of safety and food. Almost any food source can be part of their diet, and they don't need much.'

'Then they'll make it,' said Anna.

'Maybe.'

'Why only maybe?'

'Your friends. Once they know the birds are here, they'll be back to recover them.'

'Not if they never know.'

'You won't have to tell them; they will know. Everything you do here is recorded and processed. It will be uploaded as soon as you're out of this subway and on the surface.'

Anna touched the body-cam unit on the flight suit, a few inches below her left shoulder.

'Even if you destroy that, the information from your previous visit is stored with your ship's AI,' Humbro continued.

Anna checked her watch. There was ten minutes remaining before the planetary evacuation corridor would be sealed, ending all hope of departure from Earth. The past, present, and her future dreams collided and coalesced.

'Then I'll stay.'

Her words hung in the air as she stared at Humbro. The robin was still perched on the droid's outstretched hands, it chirped a high-pitched medley of notes. The droid turned towards the bird.

'It said you should leave,' the AI said.

Anna gasped. 'You understood it?'

'On a rudimentary level. The professor and I made some progress.'

'That's…'

Humbro cut her off. 'You must go now, if you are to make it.'

'But what about Artemis, when they find out.'

'Go.'

Anna's eyes narrowed.

'Then there's something you should know,' she said. 'Once the evacuation corridor is sealed there will be an electromagnetic pulse bombardment across the entire planet. Every inch. It'll destroy all electronic and electric infrastructure, and every rogue AI left. Down here you should be safe. But you must stay at this level for the next seven days.'

She flicked her gaze from Humbro to the robin.

'Tell it I'm sorry for what we've done.'

'Go,' the droid said.

Anna turned and walked along the platform, quickly breaking into a jog until she reached the stairs, which she gapped up three at a time. Her eyes adjusted to the near darkness. The route to the outside felt automatic. By the time she burst through the hole in the wall and out into the toxic air of the desolate metropolis her breathing was strained. There was no time to reboot into the exoskeleton suit. She left it abandoned on the sidewalk as she bounded along the dust-covered avenue to the scramjet.

Strapping into the pilot seat, she instructed Sheean.

'Full speed to evacuation corridor. How long do we have?'

'Seventy-three seconds.'

'Can we make it?'

The scramjet rocketed into the hazy grey clouds before powering forward. It shook and rocked as it accelerated through a succession of sound waves. In her peripheral vision, Anna saw the stormy, gyrating cloud systems fade from view.

'Passing through corridor now,' Sheean informed.

The deep blue of the Earth's atmosphere vanished, replaced by the inky blackness of space. Anna was lost in her thoughts until Sheean alerted her to an incoming communication. It was Artemis Control. A blue light blinked on the console. Anna reached to connect then paused, her finger hovered next to the pulsating light.

'Sheean. Erase all records from the dead zone.'

There was no response.

'I know; it's procedural irregularity.'

The AI remained silent.

'I can't force you, Sheean.'

Anna waited, then added, 'You know what's in the data; what it means.'

She focused on the communication button and its hypnotic pulsing light. In the corner of her right eye a tear welled.

'Done,' Sheean replied.

ABOUT THE AUTHOR

Scott Neil is a writer and journalist. He studied in England and the US and worked on regional newspapers in the UK, including Bournemouth's Daily Echo. He spent 16 years at Bermuda's national newspaper The Royal Gazette.

Other titles by the same writer:

Fiction

Dolphin Girl (2015)

Non-fiction

Eating Clouds (2008)

Lennon Bermuda (2012)

If you enjoyed this novella, please consider leaving a review on Amazon, Goodreads or any other book review site.